PATH OF BONES

A CASSIE QUINN MYSTERY

L.T. RYAN

with

K.M. ROUGHT

LIQUID MIND MEDIA

PATH OF BONES

A Cassie Quinn Mystery: Book One

L.T. Ryan with K.M. Rought

Copyright © 2020 by L.T. Ryan, K.M. Rought, and Liquid Mind Media, LLC. All rights reserved. No part of this publication may be copied, reproduced in any format, by any means, electronic or otherwise, without prior consent from the copyright owner and publisher of this book. This is a work of fiction. All characters, names, places and events are the product of the author's imagination or used fictitiously.

THE CASSIE QUINN SERIES

Path of Bones

Whisper of Bones

Symphony of Bones

Etched in Shadow

Concealed in Shadow

Betrayed in Shadow

Born from Ashes

Love Cassie? Hatch? Noble? Maddie? Get your very own L.T. Ryan merchandise today! Click the link below to find coffee mugs, t-shirts, and even signed copies of your favorite L.T. Ryan thrillers! https://ltryan.ink/EvG_

1

The sun's rays pierced Elizabeth's eyelids like serrated knives. She blinked against the pain until the blurriness faded and the world came into sharp focus. She laid on the ground, staring straight into the sun which hung bright and golden in the sky above her. She could see the treetops in her peripheral vision. They swayed in a breeze she couldn't feel.

Why wasn't it cooling her flushed skin?

Between one second and the next, her confusion faded, replaced by an immense pain radiating throughout her entire body. It ravaged her nerves, from the tip of her toes to the top of her skull. Its strength gathered in her chest. No amount of deep breathing eased the agony.

Panicking, Elizabeth sat up too quickly. Her head spun and her stomach lurched. Although the pain didn't fade, a new sensation arose. Sound came rushing back to her ears and she listened to the cacophony of the world for the first time in what felt like eons.

She scrambled to her feet despite the dizziness and walked backward until she hit a tree. She realized she couldn't feel the roughness of the bark, but the thought was driven away by the torment in her body. At the very least, leaning against the tree gave her shaky knees a break. She put her hands over her ears. She was so overwhelmed with awareness that all she wanted to do was scream.

Her mouth twisted open in wretched agony.

But no sound came out.

She grasped at her neck, squeezing as if to make sure it was still there. She took another deep breath, and the pain in her chest flared. She tried to cry out again, but her voice had been taken from her.

The sound around her started to even out, and the murmuring of voices reached her ears. Amidst her panic, Elizabeth grasped onto the sound, and for the first time since opening her eyes against the sun, she took in her surroundings.

It was a madhouse. There were at least a dozen people scrambling this way and that, taking pictures, searching the ground, or whispering over steaming cups of coffee. How could she not have noticed? They all seemed to be revolving around one singular object in the center of a small clearing in the woods.

No, not an object.

A body.

Elizabeth's first instinct was to run away from the horrid sight, but her limbs would not cooperate. Instead, she felt her feet moving forward against her volition, her curiosity outweighing her terror. When she was close enough to see the body through the haziness of her vision, realization dawned on her. All the air in her lungs fled her chest, and the dizziness returned.

Through her tunnel vision, Elizabeth could make out the small black heels strapped to the lady's feet. The denim shorts with artistic holes that cut the front. A bright pink shirt that had been stained a deep red. Elizabeth's eyes skipped over the bloody mess in the center of the torso and traveled to the pale face that she could—in some distant part of her mind—recognize as her own. Her eyes traveled back to the body's chest, her own chest. She couldn't look away if she wanted to. A gaping hole gave way to a ruby-tinted blackness and, only a few inches above that, an angry gash circled her throat like a gruesome necklace.

The sight of her wounds caused flashes of memory to erupt inside her mind, compelling her to stumble backwards.

She saw a man and a knife. She remembered what it felt like to beg for her life, only for it to fall on deaf ears. She could still feel the pain of the blade against her throat as it ripped into her flesh.

Pinpricks of tears formed in her eyes but didn't fall. She looked down, first at her own hands, then at her chest, not knowing what to expect. She wasn't translucent like the ghosts she had seen in movies. But she also wasn't corporeal. She glitched in and out as though she was nothing more than the personification of poor reception. The embodiment of static. Sometimes she was whole. Other times, she faded away. As though she were nothing but a memory.

More than ever, Elizabeth wished she could cry. She wished she could scream. She felt the emotion building in her chest, amplifying the non-subsiding pain. It was more than a constant dull ache. It was like walking around covered in acid. Every nerve in her body was on fire and there was no way to put out the flames.

The sounds of the world around her ebbed and flowed in time with her glitching. Her mind was in chaos, still wrapped in confusion over the scene of her own body. When she concentrated every fiber of her being on the people examining her corpse, she could hear what they were saying.

"Just like the others?"

"Exactly the same."

"God, I hope we can get some evidence this time."

"We're still looking, but I wouldn't hold your breath."

"You need to work on your optimism."

"Hard when your first appointment of the day is with a serial killer's handiwork."

The words "serial killer" broke Elizabeth's concentration. Those flashes of memory returned. The man. The knife. The pain. She shook her head and the memories faded, but the conversation was still muffled. She took a step closer, forcing her mind to block out everything else.

"Any leads?"

Elizabeth stared at the person speaking. He was a middle-aged man with a bad comb over. He may have been handsome in his youth, but he had let himself go. Pudgy around his middle and more than a five o'clock shadow. This was the one who had been pessimistic. The one who had uttered the words Elizabeth was desperately trying to keep out of her thoughts.

"One. It's a long shot, but I'm desperate enough to try anything."

"You gonna let me in on it?"

"Yeah, if it leads somewhere."

The second person was a woman. She was young, about five years older than Elizabeth. She was fit compared to the man. She had pulled her dark hair back in a tight ponytail and wore a dark, nondescript baseball cap. Elizabeth could tell by looking at her that she took her work seriously. Would this be the woman who would solve her murder?

Murder?

Murder.

The thought entered Elizabeth's mind unbidden and her concentration broke for a second time. It surprised her she could feel anything beyond the pain in her body; a sense of exhaustion made her want to let go and fade out of existence.

But she refused. She couldn't disappear while her killer was still out there, living his life like he mattered more than her. Anger swept across her body, almost enough to drown out the pain. She tried to cry out again to no avail.

She paced the crime scene, looking at each person's face, catching snippets of conversation here and there. She didn't understand most of it when she could hear them, but it didn't matter. They knew where she was, and that was the important part. They knew she had been killed. They wouldn't rest until they found her killer.

And neither would she.

Her determination to stick around until they solved her case lit another fire in her. This one cooled her anger, though it didn't dull her pain. Instead, she felt a strange sensation within her chest. It went deeper than her heart, deeper than her spine. It was like a rope had been lassoed around her soul and cinched tight. It wasn't painful, but it wasn't something she could ignore. It began tugging her away from the crime scene.

Elizabeth's thoughts were still frantic. It took an immense

amount of effort to think. She was dead. It wasn't easy to accept, but she had no other choice. And something was dulling the attachment to the flashes of memories that struck like lightning every few seconds. The evidence was right in front of her. Literally. Was the lasso trying to lead her to the next life? She didn't see a light other than the sun. No angels came down to escort her to the beyond. She didn't feel a sense of peace washing over her.

Were all those stories a lie? Was she going somewhere else? She pondered the questions while her feet dragged her forward. She resisted at first, anxious not to leave her body behind. What would they do with her? Would she ever see herself again? Did she want to?

Maybe the lasso was pulling her home, to her empty apartment. Or maybe it was pulling her to her mother and father and sister. Maybe it wanted her to say goodbye to her family. She dug her heels in. She didn't want that. Not yet at least. She didn't want to see them crying over her. She didn't want to see them begging for answers. She wanted to have those answers before she let go.

The lasso gave her a light tug, enough to get her moving again. She stumbled forward, through the trees and out onto a road. Cars zipped by, unaware that a few hundred feet in the woods was a dead woman staring up at the sky with sightless eyes, her heart having been cut right out of her chest.

Elizabeth looked at the sign in front of her. It faded in and out of view, but a few seconds later, she figured out what it said. She had driven along this road countless times. And when the lasso gave her another tug, she didn't hesitate. She still didn't know what she was supposed to do, but she knew where she would find her answers.

It was taking her back to the city.

Back to Savannah.

2

Once again, Cassie caught herself smiling when no one was around. She found it strange to be aware of her own happiness, to have its mere existence surprise her. She had experienced darkness for so long that the slightest of light caught her off guard.

She allowed herself to live in the moment, something she had struggled with most of her life. She would not take that feeling for granted again. It filled her with a warmth that brought a flush to her cheeks.

It had been over ten years since that fateful night in the graveyard, the one that had almost taken her life. In fact, according to the doctors, it *had* killed her. But by some miracle, or maybe her own strength of will, she clawed her way back to the land of the living. And everything changed.

The thought of her would-be killer, Novak, was almost enough to snuff out her happiness.

Almost.

It started with Novak escaping jail and going on a killing spree. That was not a great start. He had seen her picture in the newspaper and decided to finish what he had started years ago. It would've been a gruesome ending for Cassie if Mitch Tanner, a detective and friend from Philadelphia, hadn't saved her life. It was a miracle he was there.

The rest of the year had been a whirlwind of cops and trials and statements and media. The officers assigned to her case had kept her name as low profile as possible, but it was hard to go completely undetected. Still, she managed to keep her face out of the news. After all, this was Savannah. A few weeks went by and some other tragedy caught everyone's attention. She was old news.

And as crazy as her life had been, it was all worth it. Novak had been given the death penalty. The evidence against him was overwhelming, and his recent escape proved he could not be reformed. If given the chance, he would kill time and time again.

Four months ago, they had taken his life. It was a small consolation for the number of lives he had taken himself.

Cassie hadn't known peace until that day. She worried she would see him in her dreams, or while she was awake. But as the days slipped away, so did her worries. He didn't come to her, and she knew he had received the sentence he deserved.

Her face started to ache from smiling so much, but she relished the pain. It had been a long time since she had felt this light and carefree. And she would do anything to hold onto the feeling forever.

"Today's going to be the day."

Cassie was shaken from her reverie by Magdalena's voice, but she was so deep in thought she couldn't comprehend the words. The world came back into focus and she remembered she was supposed to be looking for shipping papers at the museum's front desk. Tonya ran to the break room to get some coffee. She yelled something about her kid keeping her up half the night.

"Huh?" Cassie asked, as she didn't hear what Magdalena had said.

Magdalena placed a newspaper on the counter between them and leaned closer. "Today's going to be the day. Jason's going to ask you out."

Cassie rolled her eyes. "You say that every day."

"Yeah, but I have a good feeling about today."

"You say *that* every day, too."

Still, Cassie couldn't help but glance at him. He was standing in the middle of the atrium with an elderly gentleman, explaining the best way to navigate the Savannah College of Art and Design's Museum of Art's many halls. His broad shoulders and six-foot tall frame made him look imposing, as did his security uniform. But his chocolate eyes and warm smile had a calming effect on everyone. Maybe that was what made him so good at his job.

"I see you staring," Magdalena said.

Cassie waved her off. "How's the hubby?"

Magdalena tossed a handful of braids over her shoulder and leveled Cassie with an intense stare; Magdalena knew Cassie was trying to change the subject. Luckily for Cassie, Magdalena didn't press her. "He's okay. The chemo is taking its toll, but I think we're getting through the worst of it." Her eyes glazed over but brightened again a second later. "He loved those lemon bars you made him. You keep baking like that, and he's going to divorce me."

"And risk never having your macaroni pie again? I doubt it."

Magdalena was another bright spot at the museum. She was a few decades older than Cassie, but always had at least ten times the energy. Cassie swore Magdalena never wore the same outfit twice, and there wasn't a drab article of clothing in that woman's wardrobe. No one could ever guess what she would wear on any given day. Today, it was a patchwork skirt of orange, purple, and white, topped with a yellow blazer and a simple white blouse underneath. She wore a chunky necklace, huge hoop earrings, and rings on almost every finger. And yet, she didn't look outlandish or gaudy. She could pull off anything.

If Jason had a calming effect on everyone, Magdalena was always ready to get them pumped up for the day. That was why she was the coordinator of museum visitation. She knew how to handle people.

She had a way of looking into someone's soul, just as she was doing to Cassie. "And how are you doing?" Magdalena asked.

"I'm fine."

"You know that doesn't cut it with me." Magdalena snapped her fingers. "Spill."

Cassie took a deep breath. It had been four months to the day since Novak had been put to death. Magdalena was one of the only people in Cassie's life who knew the entire story. Or almost the whole story, at least. She knew Cassie had almost died—twice—and that her attempted killer had finally paid the ultimate price for his crimes.

Magdalena didn't know about the ghosts, or that they all vanished the moment Novak took his last breath. But Magdalena was intuitive—maybe not like Cassie, but she did have a knack for reading people. Which was why she was always bugging Cassie about Jason.

"I'm good," Cassie said. She formed the words slowly to make it seem like she thought about the answer. It was close to the truth. "Things are getting easier. I'm starting to trust that it's over. My life today is a lot easier than it was a month ago."

"That's all we can hope for."

Magdalena reached out to rub Cassie's shoulder, but she let her arm fall. She knew Cassie still had trouble with people touching her, specifically her scars. Cassie offered an apologetic smile, but Magdalena waved it away.

"We're all works in progress," Magdalena said, "right up until the day we die. You've been through more than most. You deserve to be happy. Don't ever forget that."

Cassie nodded but couldn't speak. A sudden well of emotion caught in her throat and she had to swallow it back down. It was not sadness or happiness, but a strange combination of the two. So much of her life had been taken from her because of her encounters with Novak, but it had also allowed her to help many people. She couldn't erase her nightmares without erasing her dreams, too.

But that was in her past. Novak would never hurt her again. She could start rebuilding the life he had destroyed. And that had all started with this job. She hadn't been working at the SCAD Museum of Art for long, but it already felt like home. With her art history degree from the Savannah College of Art and Design giving her an "in" at the museum, she landed a position as an art preparator. Working with artifacts and displays was more than she ever could've hoped for at this time last year.

Maybe someday she would become a curator, but she still had trouble looking that far in the future. She had spent so long staring death in the face it was sometimes difficult for her to remember she was allowed to live.

Magdalena clicked her tongue, and Cassie saw she was staring at the front page of the newspaper.

"What is it?"

"Have you heard about those women who keep turning up dead?"

"Yeah." Cassie felt another lump rise in her throat, but it was nothing like the last one. "Did they find another one?"

Magdalena nodded. "Twenty-eight years old. Can you believe that? Had her whole life ahead of her. And some jerk snatched it away just because he could."

Cassie shivered. She knew what it felt like to be one of those women. Novak had made her feel so powerless. She hadn't understood fear until she came face to face with him, twice. It pained her to imagine someone else going through that, too. And they hadn't been as lucky as she had. Though some might argue they had been luckier. They didn't have to live in this realm with the knowledge of what it was like to be a survivor. To carry those memories forever. And for Cassie, it had been worse. All their psychic energy weighed down on her. At least, it had. Things were different now.

"Look at me runnin' my mouth," Magdalena said, folding the paper in half. "You need to say something when I get going or I'll never stop."

"It's fine," Cassie said. When Magdalena leveled her with another look, Cassie reached over and patted the woman's hand. "Really, it's fine. I can't go around scared for the rest of my life. That's what these last few months have been about. Fortifying myself against the world."

"Don't fortify yourself too much." Magdalena cast a significant glance over her shoulder.

"What was that you were saying about talking too much?"

The woman let out a belly laugh as her phone chimed. When she dug it out of her pocket, her smile faded.

Cassie already knew what it was about, but she asked anyway. "Is something wrong?"

"It's Roger. He's not feeling well. Sorry, Cassie. I know this is a big day for you, and we had dinner planned and everything—"

"You've got enough to worry about without worrying about me, too, Mags. Take care of your hubby. We'll go out when he's feeling better."

"Are you sure?" She leaned in closer. "You could always come over to our place. I know you don't always like to be home alone."

"I'm *sure*." Cassie plastered on a smile she hoped was convincing. "I'd get in your way. Let's try again next week."

"Next week," Magdalena said, tapping away at her phone. When she looked up again, she had a devilish look in her eye. "You could always ask Jason."

"Maybe I will."

Magdalena patted her hand before taking the newspaper and heading to her office. They both knew Cassie was lying, but neither one of them would say so. That's what friends were for and Magdalena had proven to be a good one over the last few months.

With her evening plans canceled, Cassie had trouble feeling excited about what the day had in store for her. A few minutes ago, she was looking forward to unpacking their new shipment of Vera Wang accessories and meticulously cataloging each and every one of them. Now, all she could think about were the extra hours she would be spending at home. Alone.

It was strange how a bad piece of news could snatch that newfound happiness away like it had never existed in the first place.

Cassie gathered the shipping papers she had been searching for, her heart heavy with anticipation. Even Jason's kind smile as he passed by wasn't enough to lift her spirits.

Today was not the day.

3

Cassie used her hip to shut the car door, then hit the lock button on her key fob until she heard the beep. She took a deep breath but refused to look at the front of her house yet. Instead, she stared up into the night sky, willing the clouds to clear so she could catch a glimpse of just one star. But it wouldn't have mattered. When the evenings were clear, light pollution still made the sky hazy and gray.

Still, she embraced the feel of the night air as it blew through her auburn hair, causing a few strands to tickle her cheeks. She wasn't an outdoors kind of person, but there was something special about the night sky that made her want to spread a blanket out on the grass and be one with the universe.

Cassie waited a few more seconds and lowered her gaze to the front of her house. It was an unassuming, Southern-style bungalow with gray siding and red trim. Although it was small compared to most other houses on the street, it was the perfect size for her and had a guest bedroom. Not that she ever needed it.

Cassie placed her hand on the front gate and passed through the entrance, letting it swing shut behind her. When she heard the *click* of the latch, she walked across the stone pavers with measured steps. Up the stairs. Onto the porch. In front of the door.

She had always loved her door. It was a deep red garnet. It was bold without being garish. The right touch to make her house stand out amidst the boring whites and beiges of her neighbors.

Cassie knew she was stalling, but the time had come. She took out her keys, jingled them once, and stuck the correct one in the lock and twisted. When she heard the bolt slide, she turned the handle and pushed open the door.

And right on cue, her house guest greeted her.

An angry meow pierced the air, and, despite her mood, Cassie couldn't help but smile.

"Hello, Mr. Apollo." Cassie was subjected to another piercing meow. "I know, I know. I'm late. I took myself out to dinner tonight. I had plans to go with Magdalena, but Roger was sick again."

Apollo's bright green eyes stared at her from the darkness. The orange and white patches on his face seemed to glow in defiance of the jet-black parts of his body that blended into the shadows. He blinked at her once and trotted forward, brushing himself along her legs. He forgave her and Cassie was content to run through her entire day with him, from the conversation with Magdalena in the morning, to cataloging the Vera Wang pieces in the afternoon, to the fact that Jason had waited ten minutes for her after his shift had ended so they could walk to their cars together.

"He said he had been finishing up paperwork, but I know for a fact that isn't true. Tonya at the front desk says he hands in everything half an hour early and does one more sweep of the museum until the night shift arrives."

Cassie rattled off whatever came to mind, and Apollo responded with various intonations of his meow whenever she paused to take a breath. She knew he was looking for his dinner and maybe a couple of treats, but part of her liked to believe he enjoyed the sound of her voice, too.

And it was better than listening to the dead silence of the house.

For the rest of the evening, Cassie moved from room to room, watering plants and washing yesterday's dishes and tidying up spots she had already tidied up yesterday. She kept herself busy, all while talking to Apollo or humming whatever song had been playing on the radio during her drive home.

Anything to avoid her bedroom. Anything to tire herself out so she'd be able to fall asleep. Her bedroom was the one area in her house that defied the rules the rest of her life had followed over the last four months. The one area that held the anomaly.

That's what she had been calling it, anyway. *The anomaly.* Like giving it another name changed what it was.

It didn't.

But it was midnight, and she would have to be up in six hours. There was no avoiding it. She looked down at Apollo, who responded with sleepy eyes and a yawning meow, and made her way to her room. It was always a few degrees cooler in there. It was nice during the hot Savannah summers, but Cassie wasn't sure the tradeoff was quite worth that perk.

Apollo stopped at the threshold to her room and stared into the corner Cassie always avoided looking at. Instead, she washed her face, brushed her teeth, and changed into a pair of shorts and a tank top while keeping her back to the southern wall of her room.

Not that it mattered. Ghosts didn't care if you wore clothes or not. She wasn't sure if they saw her the way humans saw her. Did she glitch in and out while they stayed static? Was she a hologram to them? Could they see through *her*?

Cassie peeled back her comforter and crawled under the top sheet, fluffing her pillow into the perfect shape. Apollo stood guard at her bedroom door. Her uninvited guests didn't alarm him, though there had been exceptions. She'd had him long enough that he was accustomed to all but the angriest of spirits. But there was something about this one that had made him reluctant to get close.

Settled into her usual spot, Cassie forced her gaze to the corner of the room she had been avoiding. It was her nighttime routine. She called it her very own brand of exposure therapy. Ghosts hardly scared her or took her by surprise these days, but she'd gotten so used to their absence over the last few months that when this one showed up at random, it was like she was starting from the beginning, back when she was learning ghosts were real for the very first time.

As Cassie's gaze found the boy in the corner of her room, their eyes locked. He always stood there, pressed up against the wall, his arms hanging loose at his sides. He was almost solid. She could still see the wall through his head, even in the dark. He never broke eye contact and he rarely blinked.

He was dressed in an oversized t-shirt and neon shorts, clearly from the '80s. The colors were dull, but not from age or use. That's how most ghosts appeared—like the color had been drained from their skin, their clothes, their souls.

The boy was maybe eight years old. If he were any older, he'd have been tiny for his age. He never spoke to her. At times, it was a relief. And at others, it was maddening. She had no idea what he needed from her, and she didn't know why all the other spirits had faded when he had not.

She spent ten years seeing and speaking for the dead, but Cassie couldn't land on a set of rules for the otherworld. Some spoke in words, while others spoke in images. Some could move objects with ease while others passed through everything they touched. Some refused to move on until she helped them, while others faded away before she had the chance.

The little boy didn't break eye contact, and Cassie knew he wouldn't. She gave him a few minutes, hoping and dreading that he might say something. But he stared and stared and stared.

She shifted away from him and closed her eyes. As she fell asleep, her mind drifted from one memory to the next. Magdalena and Jason filled her with a warmth she tried to hold onto, but she could still feel the spirit in the corner of the room staring at her. The inability to wish him away cast a deep shadow across any happiness the day had brought her. And she knew tomorrow would be the same. So would the next day. And the next.

When Cassie slipped into a restless sleep, she didn't dream. She hadn't dreamt in months. The portents that had once filled her nights were absent.

She saw and felt nothing at all.

4

He stepped out of his car and looked up at a sky littered with stars. Out here in the country, he could breathe. The clean air energized him. Nature connected him to the world. To the entire universe. He could do anything he wanted. Nothing could stop him.

No more fear.

Not even death could stop him.

He circled his vehicle and opened the rear passenger side door. In the back seat sat a large plastic storage container. The kind with handles on each end that flipped up and secured the lid in place. He had learned a thing or two since the first time, including how important it was to make certain everything stayed cool for as long as possible. He had to complete all his tasks before deterioration, and there was always so much to do.

Unable to help himself, he popped open the lid. On one end was a covered bucket, and on the other was a small, empty container. Seeing the dash of red on the inside of the plastic made his heart beat faster.

This was the answer to all his problems. This would grant him the freedom to look up at the stars for years to come.

He restrained himself from opening the lid to the bucket despite an incessant need to make sure everything was safe. This time had gone smoother than the last. His learning curve no longer hindered the mission. He was now working toward mastery.

With that skill came a calm he couldn't put into words. It was faith in himself and trust in the outcome. He had no other option but to believe this would work. Anything else would have been quitting.

The very idea left a bitter taste in his mouth.

He secured the lid back in place, snapped the handles closed, and lifted the container out of the car. The weight of it always surprised him. The human body was a miraculous system. When he was finally free of the ticking clock that carried him closer to the end, he would do his part to learn more. He had much to accomplish yet.

The stairs leading up to the front of the house did not pose a problem. The steps descending to the basement always made him wary. They were steep and narrow and bowed under the additional weight of the container he carried down. He would fix that in due time.

Setting the container on the ground, he looked over at the table he had set up against one of the concrete walls. Everything had been in place for a while, but he was compelled to go through the list of items again.

Two candles were lit, and he was about to light the third. A dagger waited, hidden under the table, until it was time for it to fulfill its purpose. The lines he had drawn on the wall in his own blood were starting to darken and fade. Now was the perfect moment to refresh them.

His phone buzzed in his pocket. A calm apathy replaced a split second of annoyance. He checked the message and allowed himself to smile. Everything was going according to plan.

"Three down," he whispered to no one. "Four to go."

5

Cassie's eyes were open before her alarm went off. She felt the gaze of the boy in the corner of the room like a thorn in her skin but refused to look in his direction. Like most mornings, she anticipated his energy. Today was a new day, and that always replenished the positivity her evenings had drained from her. There was something about the sun shining in the sky, the heat in the air, the breeze amongst the trees. It felt like hope.

Maybe today *would* be the day.

When she picked out her clothes, Cassie tried channeling Magdalena. Her wardrobe was full of black and gray and navy, but she reached into the depths of her closet to produce a bright yellow blouse. Unlike most of her wardrobe, it was more revealing. The tips of her scars would be visible along the neckline. Cassie pulled it on over her head anyway.

Throughout the year, she was prone to wearing long sleeves

and full-length pants. The heat seldom bothered her, and her fingers were always as cold as icicles, even on the hottest of days. But today was a new day, and she was ready to start fresh. She *wanted* to start fresh.

She turned to Apollo and held her arms out wide. He meowed his approval.

The drive to work was uneventful, as was her arrival at the SCAD Museum of Art. She greeted Magdalena and Jason and Tonya on her way in. The museum seemed brighter, and the warmth of her coffee spread through her chest like the gentle touch of an old friend. Though she couldn't help but tug up her shirt every few minutes, she felt powerful and beautiful and determined.

But she only had about two hours of peace.

A knock on her office door startled her, but she forced her voice to steady as she yelled, "Come in!"

Jason entered, looking sheepish. "Sorry to bother you."

"Oh, it's okay." Cassie's voice was less steady. He had never visited her in her office. Though whenever they passed each other throughout the museum they would say hello and chat for a few minutes. Her heart started thumping against her ribs, but she couldn't help the smile that spread over her face. "How are you?"

"I'm good. Do you have a few minutes or is this a bad time?"

"No, not at all. What can I do for you?"

"Uh, it's not for me. There's a Detective Adelaide Harris here to see you."

Cassie's heart skipped a beat for a different reason this time. She looked beyond Jason and noticed a tall, lean woman standing behind him. She wore a taupe pantsuit that complemented her bronze skin. Her chestnut hair was pulled back into a severe ponytail, and she looked as though she never smiled while on the job.

Cassie wasn't sure what to do.

Detective Harris stepped forward. "I apologize for bothering you at work, Ms. Quinn, but it couldn't wait. Would you mind if we talked for a few minutes?"

"Uh, sure." Cassie's heart felt like it would burst out of her chest, but she kept the forced smile on her face. "Thank you, Jason. I'll take it from here."

"Let me know if you need anything." He paused in the doorway, looking between the two women and, satisfied that Cassie didn't need him at that moment, shut the door behind him with a *click*.

Detective Harris held her hand out. "We haven't met, but your reputation precedes you."

Cassie firmly shook the other woman's hand. The detective took a seat across from her. "In your line of work, I'm not sure that's a good thing."

"Normally it's not, but my colleagues speak highly of you."

Cassie felt her face heat up. "I'm not sure what you've heard, but I'm kind of out of the consultation business."

Harris nodded and stared Cassie down with such intensity that Cassie couldn't help but squirm in her seat.

"Unfortunately, I don't have anywhere else to turn," the detective said. There was a hint of annoyance in her voice. Or was it reluctance?

Cassie swallowed back some bile. She had known this day would come sooner or later, but she thought she would have a bit more of a reprieve. "What can I help you with?"

"There's no gentle way to put this, so I apologize for being blunt. Have you heard about the dead women in the papers? Three have been found so far."

Cassie thought back to the newspaper article Magdalena had talked about yesterday. She had caught the news a few times over the last couple of weeks, too. "Yeah. Another body was found yesterday, wasn't it?"

"That's right." Detective Harris crossed her legs and leaned back in her chair. "I was hoping maybe you could help point me in the right direction, given your--" she paused here for a brief second, as if trying to find the right word "--proclivities."

"Proclivities?"

"Your tendencies, your... predisposition."

"I know what the word means." Cassie fought to keep the annoyance out of her voice. "I'm asking what you're implying."

"I'm hoping to tap into your experience with the occult."

Cassie caught herself a millisecond before she laughed in the detective's face. "I have no experience with the occult."

For the first time, Detective Harris's confidence seemed to waver. "Have I been misinformed? I thought you talked to ghosts."

"Talking to ghosts and having a proclivity for the occult are two different things, Detective."

"Are they?"

"Yes." Cassie let some of her annoyance slip through. "Describing something as occult is a blanket term for the super-natural, the mystical and magical."

"And ghosts do not fall under that blanket term?"

"They do." Cassie measured her words. She didn't want to be rude, but she also didn't want this detective to get the wrong idea. "But that's not what you meant when you asked me that, is it?"

"No." It was Detective Harris's turn to shift uncomfortably in her seat. "No, it's not."

"I don't practice magic or make sacrifices on an altar."

"I'm sorry if I offended you." Detective Harris took a moment to gather herself. "Maybe you could enlighten me about your abilities?"

Cassie took a deep breath. She'd had this conversation countless times in the past, but it didn't get easier. Or less awkward. "I can—could—communicate with the dead. Sometimes I would get feelings about certain cases. Visions, even, where I'd see the past, their past, or even scenes they wanted to show me from the present."

"Could?" Harris asked. "Past tense?"

"Yes." Cassie swallowed hard. She swore the people two rooms away heard it. The detective had an imposing presence and Cassie felt it. "It's been some time since I've been able to tap into that side of myself."

"Does this have anything to do with Novak's sentencing?"

Cassie stopped herself from shuddering at the mention of his name. "You've done your research."

"I have. It seemed like a good idea."

"I can't know for sure," Cassie continued, "but yeah it seems like my abilities faded as soon as he died."

Detective Harris gazed at Cassie for several seconds, though it felt like hours. "And you haven't received any messages? Any communications?"

Cassie's smile was tight. She could tell Detective Harris was grasping at straws she didn't believe existed. It was clear to

Cassie that the police had no leads. They were trying any avenue they could think of, and that included her.

"I haven't seen any ghosts related to this case. I'm sorry."

Detective Harris stood. "If I'm being honest, I figured it was a long shot."

Cassie stood, too. "You don't believe what you've heard, do you?"

"I deal with facts, not rumors," Detective Harris said.

"I wouldn't consider the number of cases I've helped close as rumor."

"Luck."

"Luck can be construed as magic or mysticism."

"Touché."

"You'll find what you're looking for."

"Is that one of your feelings?"

Cassie smiled, and it was genuine. "No. It's an observation. You care about this case, about these women. I don't think you'll stop until you solve it."

Once again, Detective Harris's confidence flickered, and she let her guard down for a moment. "We don't have a lot of evidence. The crime scenes are barren. Without a lead, I'm afraid these women are destined for the cold case files."

"You won't let that happen."

Detective Harris's resolve returned to her face. She set her jaw. "No, I won't."

"If I see anything, I'll reach out."

Harris produced her card. "Please do. I'll take any help I can get. Even if it's unconventional. These women deserve to have their story told."

Cassie took the detective's card, unsure if she would ever be able to help in a case like this again. She felt surprised by how the uncertainty bothered her. She looked back up at the detective, her jaw set.

"I promise if anything comes to me, you'll be the first to know."

6

Cassie couldn't concentrate for the rest of the day. Her brain buzzed as though it was full of bees, and the incessant sound was enough to drive her crazy. Instead of coordinating the new pieces they had added to their Vera Wang collection, she spent her time Googling anything and everything she could find about the women who'd turned up dead.

There had been three so far. The papers didn't have too much information since the police didn't want their investigation derailed. They hadn't yet revealed the cause of death.

During the last press conference about the murders they had only offered the standard statement: "They were treating the investigation very seriously and focusing as much of their manpower on the case as possible." She had heard those words plenty of times and she didn't needed Harris's insider information to realize the cops didn't have much to go on.

One family had put up a reward for anyone with information that led to an arrest, but so far, the comments on their Facebook post were filled with either well wishes or conspiracy theories.

Cassie's heart broke for those left behind. What had happened to those women was inconceivable. The friends and families of the victims had to face an ongoing horror until they had their answers. It would be a long time before they would be able to make peace with their losses.

Cassie thought about her own family, which always brought about a mixture of pain and longing. After the incident in the graveyard ten years ago, her parents had rented an apartment in Savannah so they could help Cassie with her recovery. Her sister was still in college at the time, but she tried to visit Cassie as much as possible. Savannah was a long way from California, but the few times she made it back to Georgia meant a lot to Cassie.

Life was good for a while. Or as good as it could get following such a trauma. Her parents were more than happy to help in any way they could, but they couldn't have known what she was going through at the time. They wouldn't have understood that her life had changed irrevocably.

She had a breakdown and while her therapist attributed it to stress, Cassie knew it wasn't related to her recovery. But how could she tell anyone what she was seeing? They wouldn't believe her and, even if they tried to be patient and understanding, it would've broken Cassie to know they thought she was crazy.

So, she pushed her parents away. She grew distant with her sister. Whether she was trying to protect them from what she saw or trying to keep herself out of an insane asylum, Cassie still didn't know. Either way, the relationship she had with her family became superficial.

The four of them had always been close. She and her sister were good kids. They were both introverts who had always cared more about their grades than being the popular kids in school. Cassie's father was the king of dad jokes and he always trusted them to make decisions for themselves, despite his protective nature. Her mom was the kindest person Cassie knew. A woman who would do anything for her kids.

That's why it hurt so much when Cassie phased them out of her life.

These days, she texted her sister every few months, but they were not as close as they had been as kids. She spoke with her parents around the holidays and on birthdays, but the conversations were brief. Her father would regale her with harrowing fishing tales or ask how her house was holding up. Her mom was there, just listening. When she spoke, the conversation ended in tears on both sides.

Cassie hadn't found a way to explain her abilities to her family. Her parents lived in Charlotte but still had friends in Savannah, so they probably had heard the rumors about Cassie. Savannah was a smaller city, with residents who enjoyed a good gossip. Cassie's name had been in the papers enough times that folks would have had something to talk about.

If her parents had heard anything, they never mentioned it.

She hadn't told them about the latest incident with Novak. Not everything, at least. The national news had caught wind of the story, so her parents were aware of his escape, his recapture, and his sentence to death. The phone call had started with tears that time, and Cassie spent an hour or two reassuring her parents she was fine and didn't need any help. She made things worse by telling them she didn't need anything, but old habits die hard.

Her cautious optimism about her fading powers led her to thoughts of reconciliation. If she could lead a normal life, maybe they could be a normal family again, or at least try without her worrying about something happening.

Then Detective Harris showed up.

Cassie cursed and closed out of the tabs she had opened about the murders. That life was behind her. She had a chance to start over, to start fresh. Maybe she would be able to go on dates and hang out with friends and talk with her family without worrying that a ghost would appear out of nowhere and derail her life.

It wasn't like she was asking for the moon. She wanted to be like everyone else. Was that too much to ask?

With thoughts of a mundane life swirling around inside her mind, Cassie kept her head down for the rest of the day and concentrated on her work. She stayed late, both to make up for lost time and avoid any questions Jason might have for her, and to prolong her trip home to her waiting guest.

If Cassie wanted to lead a normal life, she'd have to figure out what the boy in her house wanted from her. He hadn't left her room in months so she assumed he would stick around until she solved his case. With nothing to go on except his appearance, solving his case was a long shot, but there was a familiar thrill of having a mystery to solve. She tried to squash the feeling, but it refused to be ignored.

Maybe this would be her one last hurrah.

She felt a stab of guilt as she thought of Detective Harris and the case with the dead women, but at some point, Cassie would have to move on with her life. She thought back to that morning when she felt the sense of a new dawn approaching her. Today might not have been the day Jason asked her out, but it could be the day she decided to move forward.

Cassie packed up her bag and left the museum. The night-shift security officer inclined his head in her direction, and she offered a small smile in return. He wasn't as warm and amiable as Jason, which was why he had been relegated to evenings when there were no visitors to interact with. But she had to admit it was a lot easier for her to offer him a meek goodbye than it was trying to not look like an idiot in front of Jason.

The trip home wasn't long enough for Cassie to build up the confidence to charge into her room and demand the ghost give her some sign of what he wanted. Instead, she went about her routine of staring up at the starless sky, doing a slow march toward her front door, relaying her entire day to Apollo, and cleaning an already immaculate house.

In the past, it hadn't taken much for Cassie to get a ghost to point her in the right direction. Most of them wanted their cases solved. They craved peace of mind which allowed them to move on with whatever afterlife existed for them. Sometimes it would take a day or two for them to figure out how to communicate. But once they did, there was a whirlwind of activity until they faded from view. But this little boy had been different from the beginning.

He had shown up in her room one night and was there, like clockwork, every night since. It didn't matter what day of the week it was or what time she decided to crawl into bed.

He never spoke to her and he never moved around. She

never saw him outside of her bedroom. At first, it had been a relief that he hadn't followed her wherever she went, but it became maddening. Why did he remain in the corner? Why didn't he try to communicate? Was something wrong with him, other than the obvious? Was something wrong with her?

She had tried talking to him in the beginning. But he never responded. He blinked and stared. He never so much as shifted his weight from one foot to the other. She wasn't sure he could hear her, and if it hadn't been for his gaze following her every move, she wouldn't have been sure he could see her either.

Now, she had the proper motivation. When he had first appeared, she was reluctant to interact with him, and though she had tried, she'd given up after a few days of zero communication. In the days that followed, they fell into an uncomfortable routine. He stood there and she ignored him, except for those few moments every night where she opened a narrow window of possible communication.

He had never taken it before, so she wasn't sure why she thought he would now, but if she wanted to reclaim her life, she had to try.

So, she replaced her usual level of dread with faux confidence and marched toward her room, ready to begin the process of solving his case, one way or another.

When she found Apollo curled up in the middle of her bed, she knew something was off. Over the last few months, he would enter her room on occasion. But most of the time, he stood guard at the threshold. He hadn't felt comfortable enough to sleep in there for some time.

Cassie's eyes darted to the corner of her room to see that it stood empty. Her gaze flickered to each corner, thinking she might've just forgotten which one he haunted. But they were all empty.

With her entire plan thrown out the window, Cassie pulled on her pajamas, crawled into bed, and stared at the corner of her room, attempting to will him to appear one more time.

She couldn't help but feel disappointed when he didn't.

7

Cassie was startled awake when a strange noise infiltrated her dreamless slumber. It hadn't been all that loud, but its cadence was strange enough to be out of the ordinary. It had risen above the normal hum that persisted. At first, she tried to ignore it, clinging to what little rest she was able to get that night. She hated to admit it, but the little boy's absence threw her off more than his constant staring.

What if she had missed her opportunity to help him? Plenty of ghosts had faded in and out of her life over the years, and though she always hated the idea that she might not have helped them, she could at least say she had tried.

However, she had spent months ignoring the little boy. Not only had she not helped him, but she had also worked against getting mixed up in his case. She'd gone out of her way to avoid interacting with him. What if it was too late? What happened to the spirits who left her behind? Did they try to find someone else who could help them, or were they relegated to a special kind of hell?

As these thoughts pulled Cassie closer and closer to consciousness, the strange sounds playing in the background grew louder. They came into sharper focus and Cassie realized it was one sound. One voice.

Her eyes snapped open, and she shot up in bed with such force that Apollo bolted from where he was curled up next to her feet. He let out a startled meow on his way into the hallway and disappeared around the corner.

Cassie ignored Apollo's dramatic exit and found herself once again staring at an empty corner of the room. She had a few seconds to be confused until she noticed movement out of the corner of her eye.

When she twisted around, Cassie found herself face to face with a woman holding her head in her hands, rocking back and forth. Every few seconds, the woman would flicker in and out of existence like a lightbulb on its last legs. Her voice came and went with the connection, no louder than a whisper.

When the woman looked up, Cassie saw pure anguish in the spirit's eyes.

Cassie was out of bed and down the hall before she realized what she was doing. Her body seemed several steps ahead of her brain, and by the time they were both in sync, she was already in the kitchen, leaning against the counter like it was the only thing in the world capable of holding her up.

A flurry of emotions hit her with such ferocity that her knees buckled. She sank to the ground, dizzy and exhausted. She laid her head on the floor and took stock of her body. While she was tired from the lack of sleep and her sudden jolt out of bed, the adrenaline pumping through her veins shook with energy. Her heart was pounding, but after taking a few deep breaths she managed to ground herself.

The thoughts sprinting around inside her brain were harder to control. She wasn't scared of the woman in her bedroom, but she was surprised. It had been so long since she'd seen a figure besides the little boy that her body thought the best way to handle the situation was to run away. Now that she had some distance between her and the supposed danger, she started to understand how she felt.

The first emotion to reach the surface was anger.

Why now? It had been months, and the day Detective Harris had reached out to Cassie, her usual visitor was gone and replaced by a woman she had not seen. Cassie couldn't be sure, but she would've bet money that the figure was one of the missing girls. People were murdered every day and not even one of them had come to Cassie. Was it because she had started to investigate it herself? Was it because she let herself care about the outcome of the case?

Tears sprang to Cassie's eyes as the next emotion hit her square in her chest. Sadness gripped her heart and squeezed until she thought she would explode by the sheer force of it. One shallow breath chased another until she found herself hyperventilating into the granite tiles.

Apollo paused a few feet away from her and gauged the situation, sauntering forward and nudging her head with his nose. She sobbed harder and he flopped down against her arm, purring and nudging until she was able to sit up and wipe her eyes.

The pain in her chest faded, but the panic attack and sudden drop in adrenaline left her emotionally and physically exhausted. The tips of her fingers and toes tingled.

Apollo brushed against her and offered her a sweet meow.

"Thank you," she whispered, her voice raw from crying. She bent forward to pet him and he arched his back against her touch. She could still hear his purring when she stood back up.

Cassie took a deep breath and looked at the clock. If she hurried, she could still make it to work on time. Or she could call in sick and spend the rest of the day in bed. But as tempting as that sounded, she wasn't sure she'd be able to sleep at all with the spirit of the dead woman hovering around her.

Cassie drank a full glass of water and set her mind to go to work. She returned to her room with caution and found it empty. The woman no longer being there set Cassie more on edge.

Yesterday's bravery was long gone, so Cassie pulled out a lightweight long-sleeve shirt and matching black pants. She threw on her most comfortable flats and ran a brush through her hair without bothering to eat breakfast.

When she arrived at work, Jason greeted her with a hearty hello. She tried to offer him the same energy in return, but didn't have any to spare. The crease that formed between his eyebrows was enough to make her pause and come up with something close to the truth.

"Didn't sleep well last night."

"Bad dreams?" he asked.

"Yeah, something like that."

"Anything to do with what that detective wanted?"

Cassie's mouth opened to respond, but she found herself caught between answers. If she said yes, she might have to explain why the detective had wanted to talk to her in the first place. If she said no, she would have to come up with a believable lie.

Jason shook his head and offered a sheepish smile. "I'm being nosy. I'm sorry. Ignore me."

"No, no, it's fine." Cassie took a deep breath. "It did have something to do with that. It's just difficult to talk about."

"Are you in any kind of trouble? Is there anything I can do to help?"

Jason's concern made Cassie's chest ache in a different kind of way. "I'm not in any trouble, I promise. But I appreciate the offer. Thank you."

Cassie thought she caught disappointment on Jason's face, but it was replaced with his trademark smile. "Any time, Cassie. I mean that."

Cassie retreated to her workstation. With a big cup of coffee and a protein bar, she sat down intending to stay so busy she wouldn't be able to think of anything other than what was right in front of her. Nothing else would exist for at least the next eight hours. No detectives. No murders. No ghosts.

Less than an hour later, however, there was a knock on her office door. Cassie's head snapped up so quickly she felt her neck crack. For a split second, she was terrified she might see Detective Harris standing there again. Or worse—the woman from this morning.

Instead, the collections manager, Jane Livingston, stood there with her head cocked to one side and an eyebrow raised in question. She was over six feet tall with short blond hair and red-rimmed glasses. She was a cookie-cutter replica of what Cassie always believed a female executive powerhouse would look like, but her warmth and professionalism were unlike anything Cassie had ever experienced. She didn't look down on her subordinates and always did the most to make everyone feel welcome and supported.

Jane's voice hinted at a British upbringing. "You all right? Didn't scare you, did I?"

"A bit." Cassie rubbed the back of her neck and laughed. "Sorry, I was in the zone."

"That's what I like to hear." Jane leaned against the door and offered a charming smile. "You've done a great job cataloging the new Vera shipment. Thank you."

"My pleasure. We received a lot of exceptional pieces in this time."

"I know, right?" Jane's whole face lit up. "A friend of a friend works at the Met and we got first dibs on the pieces they were looking to pass along. Might've gone over the budget, but it was worth it."

"Magdalena said it's one of our most popular exhibits, so I'm sure everyone will be excited that we've got something new to look at."

"I suppose I should thank you for that."

It was Cassie's turn to cock her head to one side. "What do you mean?"

"You've done an incredible job organizing some of our modern pieces and making sure they get the attention they deserve. You have an eye for presentation, and I appreciate how diligent you've been about keeping everything neat and clean."

"Oh." Cassie was at a loss for words. "You know, it wasn't just me. The exhibition team—"

"—has all done a fantastic job, yes. And I've told them as much. But every one of them have sung your praises. Take the compliment, Cassandra."

"Thank you."

"You sound apprehensive."

Cassie blushed. "I'm either about to get a raise or a larger workload, and I don't think it's the former."

Jane threw her head back and laughed. It was loud and raucous and contagious. It seemed too big for her lean figure, and for that, Cassie loved it more.

"Guilty as charged, I'm afraid." Jane's eyes sparkled. "You've done such a fantastic job with the modern art that I'm hoping I might have you switch gears for a few months. We're about to get a truckload of new pieces in for our 19th- and 20th-century photography collection, and I want to overhaul the whole exhibit. Do you think you could spend the next day or two familiarizing yourself with our current collection and get back to me in about a week with some ideas on how we can incorporate a couple hundred more photos?"

Cassie knew Jane wasn't asking. So, with absolute dread already filling the pit of her stomach, Cassie gave her boss the answer she was looking for.

"Yes, I can do that."

8

Cassie had been standing outside the 19th- and 20th-Century Photography exhibit for a good ten minutes when George Schafer, the museum's curator, walked up to her with ease.

"Ms. Quinn." He greeted Cassie with a smile.

"Dr. Schafer."

"Did you know this is one of my favorite exhibits in the museum?"

Cassie turned to face him. He was in his 60s, with watery blue eyes and wire-rimmed glasses that made him look both ancient and eternal. He was still in excellent shape, but his wide array of sweaters and a tendency to always carry a book in one hand made him look more at home in a cottage smoking a pipe than the modern atrium of the museum.

"No, I didn't," Cassie said. "I thought you weren't supposed to pick favorites?"

George's eyes crinkled as he smiled, and he clutched a copy

of *Frankenstein* to his chest. "True, but there's something about photography that has always captured my attention. 'A picture is worth a thousand words.' They're like little windows to other parts of the world, with real people and real places. And they've been transported here, to Georgia, for us to enjoy."

"I have a feeling there's a lesson here."

George chuckled. "A lesson? No. But maybe a question."

"Such as?"

"Why do you hesitate to enjoy these little worlds?"

That was a complicated question. This wing housed over a thousand photographs—many of which were over two hundred years old. When Cassie had applied for her job at the museum, she made it known that she wanted to work with modern pieces. Despite her concentration on the Classics in college, she told George, Jane, and the other bigwigs in the room that she was most interested in how current trends reflected the ancient foundations of art.

It was a complete lie.

Cassie needed to stay as far away as possible from anything old and historic. When her abilities were at full power, she didn't need to touch an object to pick up the tragedy, remorse, and pain of the soul attached to it. Walking through some of the older exhibits, Cassie could be inundated with spirit noise.

Not every item in the museum gave off a tragic aura, but for every two or three pieces that had no effect on her, another dozen or so would reach out to her ability and latch on until she investigated further or found the strength to push it away. It was exhausting, to say the least.

George cleared his throat, catching Cassie's attention.

"I'm a bit overwhelmed." Cassie was surprised by the truthfulness of the statement. "Art can be an intense experience for me, and I feel a lot of pressure to make sure I don't disappoint Jane. Or you."

George hummed his acknowledgment of her statement and rocked back and forth on his heels a few times. He took longer to respond than most people, but Cassie had found it was worth the wait.

"I like that art has that effect on you," he said. "I think that's what makes you good at your job, Ms. Quinn. I think it's also what makes our collection here so special. Imagine looking at a stationary object and having that fill you with emotion. What an incredible talent to possess."

Cassie smiled. It's why she fell in love with art to begin with. There was so much to analyze and feel; so much to learn when you looked at a piece of art. And every person took away something different from each piece. Their experiences, mindset, and emotions all played a role in how they interpreted what they were looking at.

"I think you should embrace being overwhelmed." George turned to Cassie who was overwhelmed by the intensity of his stare. "It will be uncomfortable but imagine how much you could learn about yourself in the process. Imagine what you could learn about the effect these photographs have on our patrons. Jane has complete faith in you, and so do I. If you're willing to try, I think you could bring something unique to this exhibit."

Cassie took a deep breath. It was shaky, but George's encouragement meant the world to her. "I'm willing to try."

"Good. That's all we can ever ask of other people." He drummed his fingers against the cover of his book. "Now, I have three meetings to attend today and I'm going to see how much of this I can sneak in between each one."

George winked at her and continued his stroll through the atrium, stopping every few feet to chat with someone for a minute or two. Everyone wanted to say hello to him. She hadn't known many curators in her lifetime, but she imagined most of them were haughty and pretentious. George was warm and welcoming in a way that made her feel like she wasn't just another employee, but a valued member of the museum team. He and Jane were the kind of bosses one dreamed of having.

That feeling was enough to make her venture forward with her chin held higher. There were a few people milling about, looking at the photographs, but for the most part, Cassie had the exhibit to herself.

She noticed how silent it was. The normal buzz of supernatural energy dissipated. It wasn't as calming as she would've expected. Instead, it felt like a void. Something was supposed to be there.

That set her on edge.

Still, she started at the front of the room and wound her way through, looking at every single photograph and reading every single plaque. It didn't take long for her to drown out the rest of the world.

The photographs took her back in time to a world not so far removed from her own. Most of the images were in black and white, but her mind tried to fill in the colors. Were the models wearing sapphire blue or ruby red? Were the trees the color of sage or did they have young chartreuse buds? Was the sky cobalt or turquoise or indigo?

Cassie was not an artist as much as she appreciated other people's talents. She couldn't draw or paint or craft, but that was why she loved it so much. She understood how difficult art could be. It would take her years—decades, even—to come close to the ability these people had.

And though photography wasn't her medium of choice, she couldn't help but cherish the way the photographer told a story. They played out like a movie in front of her eyes despite not moving. She was reminded of George's words which brought them more alive. She could hear the bells tolling from a church that stood tall in Nova Scotia. She could feel the cool breeze that accompanied a colored photograph of a couple in a red convertible. She could smell the dust kicked up by a man shoveling dirt across a series of pictures.

A hand touched Cassie's shoulder and she jumped. But when she turned—ready to apologize for her nerves—she was met with open air. She heard the quiet murmurings of people on the other side of the gallery but there was no one within sight, let alone anyone within reach.

The faint smell of blood wafted through the air, and though it was subtle, Cassie had smelled the scent too many times to mistake it for anything else. At the realization, the hair on her arms stood on end, and that half-forgotten electric buzz of energy swept over her body.

Cassie squeezed her eyes shut and took several long deep breaths. She could feel the panic rising in her chest, but she refused to give in to the feeling. Not at work. Not with other people around. She didn't want pity or kindness or attention.

She waited until the hum of energy subsided to open her eyes. No one had noticed her odd behavior, and she would make sure it stayed that way. Instead of running out of the exhibit, she walked further away from the entrance. Her concentration wasn't as absolute as it was a moment ago, but she refused to give in. She ignored the electric buzzing, she ignored the goosebumps on her arms, and she ignored the tingle along the back of her neck.

But she couldn't ignore the flickering of the lights or the silhouette of a woman who appeared when the room went dark.

Cassie looked over her shoulder. An older couple walked into the exhibit, and neither one of them looked alarmed. The lights were a hallucination made for Cassie.

Sometimes ghosts could control what happened on her plane of existence. Other times, it was like she could see through the veil to their side. She was the bridge that connected the two worlds, allowing her to walk from one side to the other without anyone knowing.

When Cassie turned back around, it took every ounce of her willpower to swallow back the scream that clawed at her throat. She planted her feet and locked eyes with the woman standing in front of her. It was the same spirit who had been bent over her bed a few hours earlier.

Cassie could see her with clarity. Her hair was wet and clung to her face in clumps. It was once dark brown, now faded and lifeless. Her face was round, and her eyes bright against her pale skin. They locked onto Cassie with an intensity she had not felt before.

Having finally been noticed, the woman's mouth opened and closed. Her lips formed the words, but no sound came out. A single tear fell from her eye, dripped down her cheek, and clung to her chin. When it was shaken loose, Cassie followed the trajectory until her gaze stopped on the gash across her neck and down to the hole in her chest where her heart should have been.

The scent of blood grew stronger before fading like it had

been carried away by the wind. Cassie returned her gaze to the woman's face. The figure was still trying to speak.

"I'm sorry," she whispered, hoping no one would see her talking to thin air, "but I can't hear you."

The spirit put her hands to her own face and let out a silent scream. She dug her fingernails into her cheeks and if she had been corporeal, she would have drawn blood.

"I'm sorry," Cassie said again. "I can't help you."

It broke her heart to say those words, but what else could she do? She was starting over, starting fresh. And without the ability to communicate with the dead, how could she ever expect to help them find peace?

"You'll have to find someone else," she whispered.

The woman stopped clawing at her face and reached for Cassie. There was a desperation in her eyes that grasped Cassie's heart and squeezed until she struggled for breath. Had this spirit found a way to physically affect her? Or had the guilt in Cassie's heart caught up to her?

When Cassie's fear forced her to take a step back, the spell was broken. The woman dropped her arm, and her shoulders sank with disappointment. The lights flickered once more, and there was a small gust of wind, like the air had been displaced by an invisible hand.

Between one breath and the next, Cassie's world returned to normal. The lights were steady, her goosebumps retreated, and the smell of blood no longer hung in the air.

The one thing remaining was the guilt gripping Cassie's heart.

9

The air inside the museum was oppressive. It was hot and stale and clung to Cassie's skin like a damp blanket. She couldn't catch her breath and the fear of having a full-blown panic attack in the middle of the museum's atrium was enough to send her vaulting out a side door into the fresh September air.

The heat outside felt different, accompanied by a breeze that swept the sweat from her skin and filled her chest with a warmth that crept outward. She could breathe out here, and a deep lung full of air was enough to chase away the demons that had haunted her seconds before.

"Cassie? You okay?"

Cassie spun around to see Jason sitting at a picnic table with a sandwich in one hand and his phone in the other. He looked concerned, but it was offset by a splotch of mustard sitting at the corner of his mouth.

"I didn't know anyone was out here." She pulled her own phone out. "I also didn't realize it was lunchtime."

Jason shoved the rest of his sandwich in his mouth and wiped his face clean. He gestured to the seat across from him. "You can join me if you want. I have another ten minutes left."

"I'm not that hungry, to be honest." Seeing a dead woman a few moments ago suppressed her appetite. She saw the disappointment on Jason's face for the second time that day, so she sat down across from him anyway. The sun felt good on her back.

"How you doing today?" she asked.

"I think I asked you first." Jason's eyes saw right through her.

Cassie took a deep breath. "Honestly, I'm not sure."

"Fair enough. Wanna talk about it?"

"Wouldn't know where to start."

"How about at the beginning? How was your morning?"

The image of the woman standing over her bed sent a chill down her spine. "Had a panic attack."

"They can be pretty rough. It took me a long time to get my anxiety under control, and I still struggle sometimes."

"I didn't know you had anxiety, too." Jason felt like more than just a coworker or someone she was interested in. He could understand her. An invisible bond connected them in a way a lot of people wouldn't understand.

Jason shrugged. "I'm getting better at talking about it but it's not always easy. I enlisted in the army right out of high school. Figured it would be a good career, carry me into my forties. Took me too long to realize that wasn't what I wanted to do with the rest of my life. Saw a lot of things that I'll never be able to forget." His gaze drifted past Cassie.

Cassie felt the urge to say sorry, to tell him she was sad he felt that way. But she hated it when people did that to her. She realized that she had no idea if Jason was at all aware of what she had gone through. Had he seen the papers? Had he put two and two together?

She didn't need to know. So, she said, "Thanks for sharing that with me."

"Welcome." His smile warmed her more than the sun had. "If you ever want to talk about what's going on, I promise I'm a pretty good listener."

Cassie's automatic response was to wave away the offer, but she wanted someone else's advice. She didn't know what to do anymore and she didn't trust herself to make the right decisions.

"I have this... situation," she said. "A friend needs help, but I'm not sure I *can* help. I'm not sure I want to. And I feel like that makes me a bad person."

"Not necessarily." His answer was easy and automatic. It loosened some of the worry in her chest. "Does helping your friend hurt you in any way? Does it make you uncomfortable?"

Cassie ducked her head and stared at the ground. "Yes."

"But you're still thinking about helping them? I think that makes you a good person."

"Even if I don't end up doing what they're asking me to do?"

"A good friend will understand you might be at your limit. We all have buckets full of different kinds of energy. Physical energy. Emotional energy. Social energy. At any given time, they could be empty or full or somewhere in between for no reason at all."

"That seems arbitrary and dumb."

Jason threw his head back and laughed. "It is. But it's how

we operate. Or, at least, how some of us operate. Maybe you have to wait until one of your buckets fills up more."

"What if my friend can't wait?" Cassie asked. "What if there's a time limit on helping?"

Jason twisted the corner of his mouth up while he thought. "You have to decide if you can still help them when your bucket isn't full. Are the consequences of depleting your energy higher than the consequences of not helping your friend?"

It was Cassie's turn to scrunch up her face. "I dunno."

"Maybe you don't have to take it on all by yourself. Is there someone else who can help?"

Cassie thought of the detective, who was so determined to solve the case. "You know, I think there is."

Jason leaned back, clapped his hands, and held them out wide. "See? There you go. Problem solved."

Cassie blushed. She felt vulnerable and silly and dumb. "I didn't mean to turn your lunch break into a therapy session. I'm sorry about that."

"I'm not." Jason looked down at his hands and smiled. "I like talking to you."

"Likewise." Cassie smiled.

"Well, that's good to hear." Jason took a deep breath and locked eyes with her again. "I've been meaning to ask this for a while, but I was wondering if you might want to grab dinner with me sometime?"

Cassie's blush deepened. She opened her mouth to answer that yes, she'd love to, but no sound came out. The image of the woman with a gaping hole in her chest returned, unbidden, to the forefront of her mind.

Jason caught the hesitation. "I didn't mean to make you uncomfortable. I thought—"

"Yes! I mean no." Cassie smacked her hand against her forehead. "No, you did not make me uncomfortable. And yes, I would love to go to dinner with you sometime."

Jason gave a nervous smile. "I'm feeling a *but* coming on here."

"But," Cassie said, "my friend."

"Ah."

The inflection in Jason's voice made her realize the assumption he made. She wanted nothing more than to hang out with Jason outside of work, but she also didn't want her unwelcome visitor to show up in the middle of dinner. She had learned not to react over the years, but they still caught her off guard occasionally.

Plus, if she could solve this case, it could mean plenty of dates without any interruptions. And that would be worth the wait.

"I'm not sure what my friend might need from me, so I don't want to make any promises I can't keep," Cassie said, proud that it wasn't a lie. "But once that's taken care of, I would love to grab dinner with you."

"Sounds like a date."

Cassie smiled. "It does."

Jason returned to work, but Cassie elected to soak up the sun for a few more minutes. She pulled out her cell and the detective's business card, which she'd kept tucked inside her phone case on the off chance she decided to reach out. Any excitement left over from being asked out had already faded away. She had a bigger mountain in front of her:

How to solve a murder when her abilities were faulty at best.

10

Detective Harris met Cassie at Lafayette Square at Abercorn and Macon Streets after work. A mother and daughter stood hand-in-hand in front of a three-tiered fountain in the center of the square. The little girl shut her eyes tight, raised a clenched fist and tossed a handful of change into the water. She lifted one eyelid, then the other. A smile crept across her face and Cassie felt the child's innocence and joy lifting the mood of the park. Even the Spanish moss waltzed in three-quarter time with the gentle breeze.

Cassie spotted Harris exiting her sedan. The detective had on a navy pantsuit and cream-colored boots. Despite her attire, Cassie was sure the detective could take down any other person in a hundred-foot radius without breaking a sweat. She was all business as she approached Cassie. Harris called out, but the sound of her voice was drowned out by the bells ringing in the Cathedral of St. John the Baptist. Recently renovated, Cassie enjoyed the cathedral from a distance. She had no idea if the work done to the building had stirred up spirits, and she didn't want to find out.

"I was glad to hear from you," the detective said.

Cassie stood and shook her hand. "Were you? I kind of got the impression you were leery of meeting with me."

To Cassie's surprise, Detective Harris looked sheepish. "You're not wrong." She took a long moment to look at Cassie, sizing her up. "I can't quite get a read on you, Ms. Quinn. I'm not sure what to expect. That makes me uneasy."

"You can call me Cassie." She shrugged her shoulders. "And to be honest, you're not the first person to tell me that."

"I'm not sure if that's a good thing."

"Neither am I."

The two women sat down on the park bench. Harris looked down at the folder in her hands but didn't open it. When she looked back up at Cassie, all her previous vulnerability had vanished. "Before I show you what's in here, can I ask, why you called me? I got the impression you didn't want to help."

"It was more that I wasn't sure *I* could help." Cassie shifted in her seat and looked down the length of the brick pathway that ran along the outer edge of the park. There were a few runners, the little girl and her mother walking together, and a couple of people walking their dogs. A young couple and their toddler sat on a blanket sharing a picnic. The little one perked up when he spotted a dog approaching. The weather was warm, but the breeze made it tolerable. "As I'm sure you know, these sorts of things can take a lot out of you."

"And by 'these sorts of things,' you mean the murder?"

Cassie held back an inappropriate laugh. "Yeah, the murder." The humor drained away. "But you chose this. I didn't. I like learning about art and history and literature."

"Yet you keep finding yourself in this position." Detective Harris held up the folder, as if to say, *you know, the murder.*

Cassie shifted her gaze back to the detective. "Did you feel like detective work was your calling?"

A wistful look came over Harris's face. "Both my father and grandfather were police officers. So were both my uncles. I never thought about being anything else."

"Does it feel right? Do you feel like you're right where you're supposed to be?"

Detective Harris met Cassie's eyes. A conviction there was tangible. The detective's voice was firm when she responded. "Yes, I do."

"I felt that way, too. For a while."

"But not anymore?"

Cassie sighed. "I know you don't believe in my abilities and you're not convinced that what I can do is real. And I'm not sure today is going to help with that."

"Why do you say that?"

"My abilities have been fading since Novak's death." It took all of Cassie's strength to keep her voice from wavering when she spoke his name. "Honestly, I thought they had all but disappeared. That is, until you visited me yesterday."

"Me?"

"You." Cassie swallowed and looked back at the young family in front of her. They looked so happy. So carefree. So ignorant of what the two women on the park bench were discussing. "Last night, I saw one of the murdered women. And again, today at the museum. That's why I called you."

"You saw one of the murder victims?" Detective Harris's voice was dubious.

"I don't know who it was, but she had a huge gash across her neck, and it looked like her heart was ripped out of her chest. The timing makes me think she's one of your victims."

Harris didn't bother hiding her surprise this time. "That information hasn't been released to the public."

"May I?" Cassie gestured to the folder in the detective's hands, and when Harris hesitated, she dropped her hand. "I don't mean any disrespect, but if you don't trust me or want me involved, why did you agree to meet with me?"

"I do trust you. Or, rather, my colleagues do." She handed the folder over. "And that's good enough for me. For now."

It was difficult for Harris to say that, and Cassie didn't take this for granted. She waited a few seconds to brace herself for what she might find inside the folder. She had been down this road dozens of times, but it didn't get easier.

Cassie held her breath as she opened the folder. She was met with a small picture of a woman paperclipped to the medical examiner's report. Her name was Hannah Williams, and she was killed three weeks ago. When she flipped the paper up, there were several eight-by-ten images of the woman's dead body in the woods with close-ups on the gash across her neck, and of her empty chest.

Cassie's stomach tightened, but she kept her face calm and relaxed as she moved to the next woman. Jessica Tran. Killed two weeks ago. She had the same slash across her neck and the same wounds in her chest. Her heart had been cut out.

When Cassie turned to the third and final victim, it took her a second to recognize the face of the spirit that had been haunting her. Found dead in the woods two days ago. Her throat was slit, and her heart carved out of her chest.

Cassie pulled the paperclipped file out and set it on top of the closed folder. She read the name out loud. "Elizabeth Montgomery."

Detective Harris's eyebrows pinched together. "You recognize her?"

"She was the woman I saw this morning. And again, this afternoon."

"How did you know her wounds?"

Cassie returned the detective's gaze in silence. She was used to this part—the confusion, the discomfort, the distrust. Sometimes she was met with anger or fear. Detective Harris had landed on disbelief.

"They were hard to miss. I didn't see them the first time. She was crouched over my bed. But when she came to me in the museum, she was standing upright. She reached out to me and tried to say something, but she made no sound."

Harris looked confused. "She's the third victim in as many weeks. They were all killed the same way. The department doesn't want me to tell the press we may have a serial killer in Savannah, but the media is asking a lot of questions."

"Are there any connections between the victims?"

"Not that we can tell." Detective Harris's voice became tight. "Other than that, they're all women, they're different ages, different races, different hair colors. Different jobs, different socio-economic statuses. Their home addresses are in different parts of the city. They have different blood types and medical histories. If I'm being honest, we haven't been able to figure out why any of them have been targeted."

"Crime of opportunity?" Cassie asked.

"Statistically, women make easier targets."

"Any sexual assault?"

"No. Which tells me there's another reason why they're being chosen. This isn't a typical case."

"You came to me because you thought there was an occult element. Why?"

Detective Harris looked up at the sky, as if she were searching the clouds for answers. "It feels ritualistic to me. Their hearts were cut out. There's a reason for that. What is it?"

Cassie stared down at Elizabeth's face. "Is there a pattern to the days they showed up dead? Any holidays? Special dates for the victims?"

Harris returned her gaze to Cassie's face, and her eyes were hard. "Look, I appreciate you trying to get a grasp of the case. I can tell you've been around the block. You're asking all the right questions."

"But?"

"But we've explored all of these options. The moon's phases, the days of the week, solar events, everything. We've explored every avenue to connect these murders and there isn't one. That's why I came to you. I was told that you could look at the pictures of the victims and get a feeling, or whatever it is you do."

Cassie slid Elizabeth's photo into the folder and handed it back to the detective. "At one point in time, I could have. But Elizabeth is the first spirit I've seen in months, other than—"

Cassie couldn't finish the sentence. The little boy who had disappeared yesterday still weighed on her, as did Elizabeth's ghost. She resigned herself to solving one murder, not two. One more case and she could be free of this life. But it was starting to feel like that was not going to happen.

"I'm not getting any readings from the pictures," Cassie said. "I don't feel anything at all."

"Does that mean something?"

"Maybe." Cassie tried to remember if there'd ever been a time when her abilities were blocked like this. Had she ever felt a void like the one she was feeling now? "But I don't think so. I might not be the person to help you solve this case."

When Harris spoke again, her words felt like a sledge-hammer against Cassie's heart. "I see."

"I'm sorry." Cassie stood up, and the detective mirrored her movements. "I wish I could help."

"That's it?" Detective Harris's disappointment was soon replaced with a mask of professional courtesy. "I understand. I assume you know not to share any of this information with anyone else?"

Cassie felt guilty. But unless Elizabeth found her voice, Cassie had nothing else to go on. "If I come up with anything, I'll let you know."

For a second, it looked like Detective Harris was about to tell her not to bother. Instead, she stuck out her hand. "I'd appreciate it."

Cassie shook the detective's hand and watched her walk away with the folder of victims clutched in her grasp. Cassie thought she might feel a sense of relief. She reached out to the detective and she tried her best.

But really, she'd done nothing at all.

11

The dying sun brought him a sense of purpose. This was a rebirth. As night fell, opportunity rose. He wasn't the type to waste time on fear or hesitation, so he pushed through the door just as his phone chimed to signal sundown.

With the bucket in one hand and the small container in the other, he bounded down the stairs and out to his side yard, hustling to the third marker from the left. He had already calculated the distances between each burial spot to make sure they were equal. The preparations had been made months ahead of time. He had thought of everything.

Setting the two containers down in the grass, he walked along the shallow trench running from his house and ending in a hole about five inches deep. The trench was still neat and orderly, and with a smile on his face, he nodded at his own handiwork. He had it all in place.

Back at the hole, he popped the lid off the small container. He took a moment to appreciate the size of the human heart.

Over the years, he'd heard it was roughly as big as a fist, but this one was smaller. It was amazing to think such a small organ could keep an entire human being alive and well.

That bitter taste filled his mouth again.

So important, yet so fragile. Why had humans evolved to be so delicate? Instead of armor, they had skin. Instead of claws, they had fingernails. No horns or fangs. No venom. They weren't large or strong or fast.

But they had brains, and that was all the advantage he needed.

Shaking himself from his own misery, he pulled the heart out and felt its cool texture against his skin. Touching a human heart for the first time had caused a chill to run down his spine. It had made him uneasy, if not squeamish. But he had moved beyond that by now and was committed to using this little organ's power to his advantage.

He placed the heart in the hole and packed the dirt down over it. The missing grass was an obvious indicator that something had been buried there, but he wasn't worried about anyone looking in on his small, unorthodox garden. His neighbors were miles away, and the surrounding woods ensured he'd be left alone.

Giving the mound one more pat, he turned his attention to the bucket. This part required patience and a steady hand. His eagerness to complete the next step of the ritual made him want to rush through it so he could return to the basement, but his iron will held him back.

There was no point in doing any of this if it wasn't done right the first time around.

He peeled the lid off the bucket and peered at the crimson liquid inside. The smell was not pleasant, but he had grown accustomed to the way his new hobby accosted his senses. He had never been a weak man, and he wouldn't start now.

Not even under the current circumstances.

The bucket strained his muscles as he lifted it, but despite the slight shaking in his arms, he poured the liquid into the trench, walking back toward the house with purposeful steps. He made sure all the blood disappeared into the dirt. Not a single drop would be wasted.

When the last of the blood left the bucket, he set the container down and watched as the earth drank up his sacrifice. He already felt lighter. Stronger. Freer.

Was there anything he couldn't do?

12

Cassie couldn't sleep that night, compounding the effect the early morning had on her brain. She wasn't sure if it had anything to do with the little boy's absence, Elizabeth's presence, or Detective Harris's disappointment.

Or maybe it was a combination of all three.

She dragged herself out of bed. Her limbs felt like they each carried an extra ten pounds. On the upside, Elizabeth hadn't shown up this morning and though Cassie wasn't ruling it out, she was hedging her bets and trying to stay hopeful. She made extra-strength coffee, packed a lunch, and headed to the museum.

It was the little victories.

But by the time she made it to the breakroom for lunch, half the staff was crowded around the small TV in the corner.

Cassie found a spot between Magdalena and Jason. "What's going on?" she whispered.

Magdalena shook her head. Jason leaned down.

"Isn't that the detective that came here the other day?"

Cassie shifted to one side so she could see the screen better. The camera zoomed in on Harris, who stood outside the precinct surrounded by reporters. She didn't look uncomfortable, but Cassie knew enough about the woman to realize she'd rather be solving the case than talking to the press.

Harris held up her hands and the camera zoomed in further. "As I've said previously, I cannot share any sensitive details about any ongoing cases. This is to protect the investigation, and the friends and families of anyone involved in a serious crime."

"Like the murder of three young women?"

The camera panned over to a young blonde woman whose curls bounced when she talked. She was tall and imposing and Cassie had a feeling she wasn't the least bit afraid of Harris's demeanor. The reporter was holding her microphone out to the detective, waiting for an answer.

"Like I said," Harris repeated, looking the woman dead in the eyes. "I cannot comment—"

The reporter didn't let her finish. "Is it true all three women have the exact same wounds?"

Harris's eyes widened for a fraction of a second. It wasn't enough for most people to notice, but the reporter narrowed in on it like a hawk. She smiled like she had won a secret competition between her and the detective. She knew she had hit close to home.

"I cannot comment on the nature of our investigations. As soon as I can share any details about any of my current cases, I will be sure to inform all of you."

The rest of the press surged forward, yelling over each other to be heard. One voice was louder than the others, and it belonged to a short man with graying hair. He wasn't as pushy as the others, but it was clear he knew how to make himself heard.

"Does this mean we have a serial killer on our hands?"

The group of reporters fell silent. They didn't want to miss the detective's answer.

"Like I said—"

"With all due respect, Detective," the man said, "people are scared. Is there anything you can tell us?"

Detective Harris sighed and looked around the crowd. For a split second, she looked into the camera, and to Cassie, it felt like Harris was speaking directly to her.

"I know everyone is scared, but please know that we're doing the best we can. I can't share any information with you because I don't want to corrupt the investigation. I'm not trying to keep secrets from you. I'm trying to preserve the integrity of the investigation."

When the voices started to shout again, she held up her hand. Cassie was impressed with the way she could command a crowd.

"My suggestion is to stay safe and vigilant, as you have always done. Don't meet up with strangers alone, and don't do anything that your gut tells you is too dangerous."

The blonde reporter's voice rose above the rest. "So, you're telling the women of Savannah that they should be afraid for their safety?"

Detective Harris kept her eyes forward and her face neutral as she pushed her way through the crowd and got into her car. She drove off, leaving the gaggle of reporters in her wake. The cameras cut to a side-by-side of the reporter outside the precinct and two news anchors sitting behind a desk.

The breakroom erupted into several different conversations, and Cassie noticed Jane discussing the news with other employees. It seemed everyone had tuned in to the broadcast.

"Those poor girls," Magdalena said. "They don't deserve to be paraded through the headlines like that. Their souls won't have any rest until that detective solves the case. Why can't the press let her do her job?"

"The press is trying to do their jobs, too," Cassie said, "but I don't disagree with you."

Jason leaned in close to Cassie. "But that is the detective who visited you the other day, isn't it?"

Magdalena must've caught sight of the panic in Cassie's eyes because she gave Jason a death glare. "If Cassie doesn't want to talk about it, she doesn't have to."

Jason looked so chastised that Cassie put a gentle hand on his arm. "It's fine. Yeah, she's the one that was here the other day. She had a couple questions, but I wasn't able to help her."

"And you're sure you're not in any trouble?" he asked.

"I'm sure. I'm safe." Cassie gulped. "I'll tell you more some other time. But not here."

"Sure," Jason said. His eyes were huge, and Cassie felt bad about the millions of theories running through his brain. "You know where I am if you need me."

"Thanks, Jason." Cassie waited for him to leave. She turned back to Magdalena. "So, he asked me out yesterday."

"And you didn't tell me!" Magdalena hissed.

"I was going to," Cassie hissed back. "I've had a lot on my mind."

"Are you going to tell him about you-know-what?"

"I'd like to one day. Kind of a difficult thing to work around for too long. But I'll let him buy me dinner first."

"Smart move. Get into his pants first." Magdalena smiled and winked and looked between Cassie and the television. Her tone turned serious. "But what did she want?"

"You know, you're as nosy as he is."

"Yes, but you *let* me be this nosy."

Cassie couldn't deny that. "I've helped out the police with cases in the past," Cassie measured each word as she said it. "I know some people downtown, so she's heard of me. I think they're pretty desperate for answers."

"I would be, too," Magdalena said. "If they're not careful, they're going to have a full-blown panic on their hands."

"I think that's what the detective is worried about," Cassie said. "Sharing details about the case might make things worse."

"Do me a favor?" Magdalena placed her hands on Cassie's shoulders and squeezed. Her eyes wavered as she took Cassie in. "Be extra careful."

"I always am," Cassie said. "Trust me, I'm the last person you need to worry about."

"Yeah, well, crazier things have happened." Magdalena looked at her with concern. "Sometimes it doesn't matter how mindful you think you are."

Cassie sighed. She knew Magdalena was right. Those kinds of thoughts could keep her up at night, but she'd been better about keeping them at bay. However, this case brought back some terrible memories.

"All right, then." Magdalena clapped her hands together. "Are we going to try to elbow our way to a table?"

Cassie looked around the room. It was still packed, and half of the other employees were still watching the news channel. "I think I'll eat in my office," she said. "It's too crowded in here."

"All right, I'll see you later, sweetie. Keep your head up."

Cassie smiled and took her lunch back to her workstation. She wasn't hungry anymore, but she forced herself to eat half of her sandwich. It was just a way to waste time though. She knew what she had to do next and, while she always enjoyed talking to the person she was about to call, she knew reaching out to him would further embroil her in the case.

She scrolled through her contacts and found his name. She hesitated, then hit the call button.

13

"Cassie? What's wrong?"

David's voice was gruff, but warm. He was a bear of a man whose bark was far worse than his bite, though he could still hold his own in a fight. Cassie had met him a few years ago on a gruesome case and over the years he'd gone out of his way to check on her. He sat behind a desk these days, but he was still one of the sharpest cops she knew and one of the few who believed in her gift.

"Why does something always have to be wrong?" She injected as much sweetness into her voice as possible. "Maybe I want to catch up with an old friend."

"You never were a good liar, Cassie." David chuckled. "But I promise my ego can handle it."

That was another reason she liked David. He was both a professional and a friend, at least to those who hadn't made it onto his shit list. When he was on the clock, he was all business. But when he went home to his wife and grandkids, he transformed into the gentlest soul Cassie had ever met. He and his wife had invited her over a few times, and it had always made her feel like she had family in Savannah when hers was hours away.

There was no point in beating around the bush. "I'm calling about the three women who've turned up dead."

David cleared his throat. "Have you seen something? I can put you in touch with the lead detective."

"Harris, right? Yeah, I've met her."

David chuckled, but there was no humor in it. "She's a great detective, one of the best I've ever seen."

"But?"

"But her bedside manner could use some improvement."

"I'll have to agree with you there." Cassie cradled her phone against her shoulder and took another bite of her sandwich. "I talked with her last night about the victims, but she seemed pretty cagey about giving me too much information. I was hoping you could fill in some of the blank spaces for me?"

David sighed. "I gotta be honest, I don't like the idea of going behind her back. Professional courtesy."

"I know, I know." Cassie put her sandwich down and took a sip of water before she continued. "I don't want to put you in a position that could get you in trouble and if I'm crossing the line here, tell me to back off. But I could use some help."

There was shuffling in the background and David's voice lowered to just above a whisper. "Why don't you tell me what you know, and I'll see if there's anything I can add?"

Cassie sat back in her chair and stared up at the ceiling tiles above her head. "I know each woman had her throat slit and her heart removed. I know their bodies were all dumped in the woods. I also know there's no connection between any of the victims, other than they're women."

"You've got most of the facts then."

"Harris sought me out because she thought I had a 'proclivity for the occult.'" Cassie paused to hear David's reaction and was not disappointed by his amused snort. "When I started asking about possible ritualistic aspects, she shut down. Granted, she was the one who came to me about that sort of thing."

"I don't think the bosses are putting much credence in her theories at the moment. To be honest, she seems to be grasping at straws."

"Do you blame her?"

David sighed. "No, I don't. I'd be exploring every option. Including you."

"You suggested my name, didn't you?"

Cassie could feel his shrug through the phone.

"I did," he said. "She had me look over the case files, but I couldn't come up with anything she hadn't already thought of. Other than you, of course."

"I'm sure that was an interesting conversation."

"She's heard about you. Hard not to around here."

"But I'm sure having a referral from the great David Klein didn't hurt."

"Now you're trying to make me blush." David drew a deep breath. "When she came to you, did you feel anything? See anything?"

"Not at first. But that night, one of the victims showed up."

"Is that the first one since…"

"You can say his name, David."

"He doesn't deserve to have his name spoken aloud ever again."

"Fat chance of that happening. They're writing a book about him." A bubble of emotion rose in her chest and she wasn't sure if she wanted to laugh or cry. She let it subside and spoke again. "They'll turn it into a made-for-TV movie."

"You sound awfully cavalier."

It was Cassie's turn to shrug. "I don't know how I feel about it. I'll never forget him, not until the day I die, but I don't need to be afraid of him either. He's gone. Maybe my story will help someone else work through their own trauma. Or maybe I'll inspire the next David Klein."

"You're a bigger person than I'll ever be, Cassie." David's chair squeaked and his voice grew quiet again. "That man deserved something worse than a needle in his arm."

"I don't disagree. But to answer your question, yes, it was the first new ghost to show up since Novak's death." Cassie felt a pang of guilt for her lie, but she hadn't told anyone about the little boy. Not even David. "And she appeared for the first time after Harris's visit."

"Interesting." He sounded animated. "That's another point for the idea that your abilities could be tied to knowledge about the victim or the crime. Maybe that ghost or whatever was hanging around Harris and sensed you could help?"

"Let's not get into your conspiracy theories, please." A long time ago, she gave up on guessing why she had these abilities. She took another sip of her water, trying to wash the bad taste out of her mouth. "Is there anything else you can tell me?"

David's silence was too long to be a normal part of the conversation. When he spoke again, his voice was quieter. "All their blood was drained. Each one of these women were bled dry."

"I'm guessing he did it from the gashes in their necks?"

"You guess right."

"That lends more credence to a ritualistic killing," Cassie said.

David blew a gust of air straight into the phone's mouthpiece. "The person doing this is choosing women for a reason, but he's not particular about his victims. It tells me he's not playing out a fantasy with one person in mind."

"So, he hates all women?"

"It's possible. The murder is not sexual in nature. If he's cutting their throats first, he's not looking to prolong their deaths and make them suffer. Then again, cutting out their hearts is a pretty brutal act."

"Does that have any kind of significance?"

"Each organ has a certain function or meaning, right? The heart symbolizes love. Or maybe it could have a specific significance to him. But without more information, there's no way of knowing what his motive is."

"And the way to get more information is to find more bodies."

"Not something we're hoping for."

"What about where the bodies were found?"

"They were all found in the middle of the woods in different public parks. He could've taken them there in the dead of night, killed them, and no one would be any wiser until the morning when their bodies were found."

Cassie sat upright. "Is there any pattern to the locations?"

"Not that I could tell." Cassie deflated, but David continued with some hope in his voice. "But humans can't truly be random. Everything we do is influenced by our behaviors, our life experiences. For example, all the squares in Savannah, or as it pertains to this investigation, all parks within driving distance."

Cassie nodded. "They live somewhere around here."

"We know most serial killers are male and the crime indicates this is true. He could be anywhere from in his twenties to his early fifties. Smart enough to get away with several murders and strong enough to carry the bodies around. He'd blend in, perhaps be average or unremarkable, but enough of an outcast that he's coping with his issues in a less than productive way."

Cassie finished her sandwich. "The first crime scene is where the most mistakes are made, right?"

"Correct. If the killer hasn't perfected their method yet, they're more likely to leave something behind."

Cassie knew she was taking a chance with her next request. "Would you be willing to give me the first location's address?"

The silence stretched on for a beat. And then two.

"The first body we found isn't necessarily the first person he killed. That person might not be amongst one of the three we have come across."

"I understand."

"This is a longshot."

"I know." Cassie wouldn't let him stretch out the moment any longer. "If I can go to the crime scene, I may be able to pick something up. I might be able to help, David."

He sighed. "I know, I know." There was typing in the background. Then a deep sigh. "You ready? And remember, you didn't hear this from me."

Cassie grabbed a notebook and pen from her desk. "Go ahead."

14

As soon as Cassie got off work, she made a beeline for Lamarville Community Park. This was where the first body had been found three weeks ago. There was a chance Cassie could get a read from the site and find some answers.

The gravel crunched under Cassie's tires as she pulled into a parking spot. The humidity broke and drizzle hung in the air. Only a few people were still out and about, which meant she wouldn't have many onlookers as she tried to find where the first woman had been killed.

Cassie took a few calming breaths and got out of the car. She didn't have high hopes she would find anything to latch onto, given that her abilities were spotty at best these days. Regardless, Elizabeth's presence meant Cassie's abilities still worked. At this rate, Cassie didn't know what to expect.

She exited the car and took in her surroundings. As she walked down a path into the trees, all outside noises were swallowed by the forest. There were no cars or laughing kids.

Instead, there were chirping birds and singing insects and raindrops hitting the leaves overhead. The crack of a stick echoed around her as a deer took off running in the opposite direction. The sun disappeared behind the canopies above her and a chill breeze made Cassie pull her hoodie tighter around her chest.

She didn't hate being outside but given her fair complexion and strange ability to attract both living and dead people, becoming one with nature had its own set of variables. Not to mention what a forest like this could keep secret. Dense woods and treacherous land were often a dumping ground for the worst kind of people.

It didn't take long for her to find the spot David described. There was a beaten path back to where the body had been dumped. Whether it was from the police or mourners, she wasn't sure. Maybe it was from people who had a morbid sense of curiosity and couldn't help themselves.

The police had found the body about three weeks ago after a pair of young teenagers playing hooky from school had decided to take a walk through the woods. The scene freaked them out. They called the cops, then left the area, afraid to get in trouble. They'd been tracked down. David had said the officers who went to interview each of them hadn't given them too much trouble given the circumstances, but they had reiterated how important it was not to try to hide from the police.

Cassie wondered how finding a dead body would change each of their lives. Would they become cops? Doctors? Killers? There was no telling.

People had laid flowers for Hannah Williams in the spot where she had been found, but they were withered and dead by the time Cassie got there. There may have been other mementos—like teddy bears or candles—but they had either been stolen or taken away. There were no other indications of the horror that had been found here.

Cassie felt the crunch of sticks and dead leaves underfoot. The scene was unassuming, to say the least. The body had been removed, and there was no indication that it had been there at all. Biohazard techs would've cleaned the site. Rain took care of the rest, washing away any remnants of blood or signs of struggle, so there wasn't much to look at. The police would've already gathered all the evidence there was to find. She wouldn't kid herself into thinking she was any better at playing detective than Harris or her colleagues.

So, why are you here? She chastised herself.

The wind answered with a sharp gust of air and Cassie closed her eyes against it.

Why *was* she there? David had said Hannah might not have been the first person this man had killed, despite her being the first body they found. The trees were too dense to navigate with a vehicle, so he had either lured her into the trees or carried her there when no one was looking. But he had covered his tracks and left zero evidence behind.

Cassie opened her eyes. *So, why this spot? What was special about this specific location?*

Despite dealing with the dead for the last decade, Cassie didn't know much about ritualistic sacrifices, if that was what this was. Still, she tried to take in the area surrounding the crime scene. She saw many oak trees which, to her uneducated eye, looked ordinary.

Cassie took a few more steps forward as another breeze blew through the trees, carrying the faint smell of blood with it. Was it because she was several steps closer to where the woman had been dumped, or would she be coming face to face with another spirit? Would it be Elizabeth or Hannah or someone else?

Cassie felt her frustration rise. On a good day, the spirit world was cagey. Ghosts appeared when they could, and they did not when they could not. It was as simple as that. But with her abilities on the fritz, she had no idea if she was having trouble tapping into the other side. The idea that she could be surrounded by ghosts and not know was worse than all the horrors she had seen over the years.

Another branch snapped to Cassie's left and she froze. She wasn't sure if she should stand still or crouch down to hide. If someone were that close, they would have already seen her, and it wouldn't make a difference what she did.

Her heart started beating in response to her chaotic thoughts.

The wind rose again, this time bringing in a stronger scent of blood. It must have been concentrated because she could smell it with more ease than she could in the museum, despite the breeze and open air. Were her powers coming back or was the spirit stronger than it had been yesterday?

Movement on her left made Cassie turn her head in time to see a figure blink away. Most people would have said it was a trick of the light, but Cassie had been doing this too long to not know what she just saw.

The creak of a tree forced Cassie's attention forward and she saw the figure again, this time brighter than she was a few seconds ago. Cassie recognized her from the folder of victims. It was Hannah Williams, the woman whose body had been dumped here in the dead of night. She was wearing a long, flowing red dress that fluttered in a wind that didn't exist.

The spirit looked at Cassie for the span of two heartbeats

and stepped forward. Another branch cracked from behind Cassie. She didn't bother checking. She didn't want to risk losing the connection she had with Hannah.

The apparition was unflinching as she strode toward Cassie. She looked stronger than Elizabeth had. She had been here longer, so it made sense. Like Elizabeth, her hair was still stringy and wet, but Hannah's was platinum colored. And like Elizabeth, she had a gruesome gash across her neck, and her heart was missing from her chest.

Instead of the fear Elizabeth had displayed, there was angry determination.

"I'm trying to help you." Cassie's voice came out in a croak and the woman stopped advancing. "But I need you to point me in the right direction. I need you to tell me something, anything. If there's the tiniest piece of fabric, skin, or even blood out here, show me."

Hannah took a couple more steps forward. She opened her mouth but seemed unsure that anything would come out. When it did, she looked relieved.

"It'll be over soon."

The words were encased in static, as though coming from a distant radio station. Hannah's voice was deeper than Cassie expected. With every glitch in her words, Hannah faded in and out of existence. Cassie hoped the spirit could maintain the connection long enough to reveal her truth.

Emboldened after making contact, Hannah took a step forward and opened her mouth again. *"It'll be over soon,"* she repeated in the same deep tone, but this time the sound had been amplified by a factor of ten.

Cassie planted her feet as she bowed back. Every cell in her body was telling her to run in the opposite direction, but that instinct hadn't served her well when she was on a case. Ghosts didn't care about distance or speed or walls. If they formed a connection to a person, place, or thing, they would find you one day. No matter where you tried to hide.

But had Hannah formed a connection to Cassie because Cassie had decided to investigate this case? Or was Hannah only linked to this dumping ground? Cassie had no way of knowing unless Hannah told her.

"It'll be over soon."

Softer. More passionate.

"I don't know what that means." Cassie tried to keep her voice steady and neutral. Heightened emotions didn't mix well with the spirit world and Cassie had only been around Hannah for a minute or two. She didn't know what kind of spirit she was. "Who are you talking about?"

"It'll be over—"

Hannah's gaze shifted to behind Cassie. Her eyes widened. The sentence died on her lips and she blinked out of existence between one breath and the next.

And when a hand fell on Cassie's shoulder, she couldn't stop the scream that ripped from her throat.

15

"It's me! It's just me."

Cassie twisted around to find herself face-to-face with Detective Harris. Her throat burned and her heart drummed against her chest. She put her hand out to steady herself. The rush of adrenaline made her dizzy, and for a second, she wasn't sure she'd be able to stay upright without help.

"Oh, God! You scared the ever-living shit out of me!"

Harris's concerned gaze turned into one of disapproval. "What are you doing out here?"

Cassie's senses came back to her and soon enough, her heart rate was back to normal. She looked over her shoulder, but Hannah was gone. When she met Harris's eyes again, they had cooled further.

"Looking for answers" Cassie said. "How did you know I was here?"

Harris had the wherewithal to keep direct eye contact with

Cassie. "I went to the museum, but you had just pulled out of the parking lot, so I decided to follow you."

"So, you're stalking me?" Cassie tried to smile but was sure it looked like a sarcastic smirk.

Ignoring Cassie's comment, Harris asked, "How did you know to come here?" When Cassie's cheeks colored, Harris's lips thinned as she shook her head while crossing her arms over her chest. "Klein. What else did he tell you?"

"He might have mentioned the victims' blood had been drained." Cassie caught the anger on the detective's face and rushed on. "Don't be mad at him. He was trying to help me. And the victims. And I'm trying to help you."

"Are you sure that's what this is?"

Cassie's blush faded, but the heat in her cheeks remained, replaced with a flash of anger. "Am I a suspect, Detective Harris?"

"At the moment? No."

"Am I a person of interest?"

"Again, at the moment? No."

"Then why are you treating me like one?"

Detective Harris tilted her head back and let out a huff of air aimed at the trees. Her lips flapped for a second or two. When she looked back down at Cassie, her eyes seemed a few shades warmer. "You want the honest answer?"

Cassie raised an eyebrow in response.

"I'm not sure what to make of you."

"You're not the first."

"I'm sure." Harris paced the clearing, deliberately kicking leaves up as she walked. "Look, I know you had nothing to do with this. You're not a suspect. But I have to be careful. We don't need a media frenzy on our hands. That's not something I want to deal with on top of everything else."

"I caught your impromptu press conference. It looks like it's going to be hard not to have the press digging into this more than they already are. I'm not trying to make your life harder. I know you have no reason to trust me, but we both know David. Does he seem like a guy who would put stock in some crazy lady who claims she can talk to ghosts?"

Harris laughed, disproving Cassie's previous theory that Harris never smiled on the job. "No, he doesn't."

"He's a good man and I know you trust him. He trusts me. So, let me help you. You came to me, remember? I didn't ask for any of this. I thought I was done. And I was okay with that."

Detective Harris moved past Cassie and while she didn't welcome Cassie with open arms, she didn't tell her to get lost either. That seemed like a win, however marginal.

"Did you figure anything out?" Harris held out her arms and wiggled her fingers. "Get any feelings?"

"Okay, you don't have to say it like that," Cassie teased. "But no, I didn't. No feelings, at least." She paused and waited for Harris to re-engage her focus. "I did see Hannah for the first time, though."

Detective Harris couldn't hide the disbelief on her face, but she went with it anyway. "Is that what was happening right before I arrived?"

"You mean right before you scared me? Yeah."

"You were muttering to yourself. I called your name at least three times."

Cassie shook her head. "I was pretty focused. She talked to me. She kept repeating the phrase '*it'll be over soon.*'"

Harris's mouth twisted to one side. "Any idea why?"

"I'm kind of hoping it's the last words she heard and not an omen of death, you know?"

"Fair enough."

For a moment, the only sounds came from the birds and insects and trees around them. There was a faint buzzing and Harris pulled her phone out of her pocket. She held up a finger and walked a few paces away.

Cassie returned her focus to the crime scene and gave Harris her privacy. The smell of blood had vanished, but the breeze still chilled Cassie in an unnatural way. There was a chance Hannah was still hanging around but refused to show herself while Harris was present. It felt good to have another living person nearby. At the same time, Cassie wanted to see if Hannah had anything else to say.

Moreover, she wanted to make sure *"it'll be over soon"* didn't have a double meaning.

Ghosts were imprints of their former selves, with a limited amount of energy to use when making contact. In all of Cassie's experiences, she found that when they spoke, it was relevant information, however it sapped their energy as quickly as physically manipulating an object. It might take days or weeks before they could reappear without access to a power source.

Sometimes, they had enough humanity left inside them to pass on messages or say goodbye to loved ones, but that was rare. Those came with older spirits. They'd hung onto the plane long enough to understand whatever physics was needed to move objects or speak to people other than mediums. They were the ones horror stories were based on. Cassie didn't have a lot of experience with that kind. By the time they had reached that point, they were less interested in helping and more interested in hurting.

Luckily, both Hannah and Elizabeth seemed like they were trying to make contact for productive reasons. If only Cassie knew what Hannah was trying to say to her.

"I'll be there in fifteen. Yeah. Thanks. Bye."

Harris walked back over to Cassie. "That was the coroner. They're going to release Elizabeth's body back to her family in the morning. I convinced the medical examiner to hold off on stitching her back up right away because I was kind of hoping you'd go down there with me."

"That's why you're stalking me?"

"You don't have to say it like that." Harris smiled again for show. "Look, I'm going to be the first one to admit that I don't believe in psychics and ghosts and all of that mumbo jumbo, but I know Klein. I've looked up to him for years. And I've seen enough of your file to know that you get results. Plus, you're kind of a spooky chick."

"I'm *spooky*?" Cassie couldn't help but laugh. "What does that even mean?"

Harris's demeanor changed and her face tightened. "You kind of freak me out, Quinn. You might not look the part, but you act it."

"Thanks? I think?" Cassie sighed. She didn't feel like visiting a morgue on a Friday night, but she did want to help Harris solve this case sooner rather than later. For Elizabeth and Hannah's sake, as well as her own. "All right. Deal. Do I at least get dinner out of this?"

Harris rolled her eyes. "If you're still hungry after we see Elizabeth, we can go to Narobia's. They have the best shrimp and grits in Savannah."

"That seems like a bold claim, but I'm willing to give it a try."

Cassie followed Harris back toward the trail. "Hey, I know this isn't easy for you."

"What? Trusting a psychic?"

"Or an outsider." Cassie wet her lips. She didn't know what she wanted to say, but she wanted to reassure Harris that she wasn't making a mistake by confiding in Cassie. "I've been doing this for a while and it still seems crazy to me. I don't blame you for being hesitant."

"I appreciate that." Harris threw a glance at Cassie and continued. "Can I ask you something?"

"Yes, they look dead. No, I can't make them go away when I wish super hard. Yes, they've interrupted some, uh, special times."

"That's not—wait a second. Are those all the questions people ask you?"

"Without fail."

"Wow." Harris looked like she was caught between wanting to laugh and feeling bad for Cassie. "You know what? I'm not surprised."

"What was your question?"

Harris's face turned serious. "Do you ever get scared?"

Cassie took her time with the question and offered a slow nod. "I would say it's gotten easier, but that fear doesn't go away, you know? There's a reason why they make horror movies out of this stuff. And while I may have seen just about anything you could think of, it is still shocking at the very least when receiving an unexpected visitor."

"True." Harris took a deep breath as her gaze drifted to the canopy overhead. Already, a smattering of orange and yellow and red leaves softened the view.

Cassie took advantage of the void hanging between them. "Do *you* still get scared?"

Harris's gaze returned to Cassie. She smiled and took a moment to respond. "Yeah. All the time. When you're around death this much, it's kind of hard not to. You want to be this hard-as-steel, tough-as-nails badass detective, solving crimes and all. But it's all a front."

"Were you hoping I'd say it would get easier? That one day you might be less scared?"

Harris shrugged. "Maybe. Kinda. Yeah."

Cassie smiled. "It's okay to hope that. I wish I were less scared, but sometimes fear is a good thing. Sometimes it can save your life. I'm sure you already know that."

"I do," Harris said. "But sometimes it's nice to hear that out loud."

"These murders, they're weighing on you, aren't they?"

"It's not easy," Harris said. "No matter who it is. But I see these women, and they're not much younger than me. We can't come up with a pattern with a reason for why they've been chosen. It's unnerving."

"Well, for what it's worth, I believe in you."

"Thanks." Harris's smile was genuine but sad. "Come on. We don't have much time."

Cassie got into her car and waited for Harris to pull out. She followed the detective onto the street and toward the city morgue.

What a thrilling Friday night, she thought.

16

The city morgue was an unimposing brick building that belied the darkness passing through its walls. Sometimes bodies were stored there while the workers awaited identification or autopsies.

Cassie hated morgues. For someone with her gift, the place could best be described as an awkward social mixer. With the undead. She had been several times, and it never got easier. Spirits often liked to hang around their bodies. Cassie could be inundated with ghosts and psychic vibes. When her gift was stronger, she could sift through them and focus on the ones who would help her solve a case.

Now, she wasn't sure what would happen when she stepped into that building.

Harris got out of her car first and Cassie followed.

"You okay?" Harris asked. "You look pale. Well, paler than usual."

"I'm fine." Cassie rolled her eyes at Harris. "This place makes me nervous. Not sure what I'm going to see inside."

"Well, I can guarantee you're about to see a dead body," Harris said. "If that helps."

"Not in the slightest," Cassie responded, but followed Harris inside anyway.

The detective introduced herself to the employee at the front desk and was buzzed through the heavy steel doors where they were met by Dr. Seth Underwood. He was a large, bald man with dark, beady eyes and a huge mustache that made him look like a walrus. His outward demeanor was all business but sidle up next to him at the bar at the Wormhole on Bull Street, and he'd keep you in stitches half the night.

"Dr. Underwood," Harris held out her hand for him to shake. "It's good to see you again. This is—"

"Cassie Quinn," Underwood ignored Harris's hand and stared Cassie down for a beat too long. For a moment, Cassie wondered if she was about to receive a lecture. Underwood's face erupted into a huge smile and he bent over to hug her. "How have you been?"

"Better." Cassie allowed the big man to squeeze most of the air out of her lungs. "How about you? Your hip still bothering you?"

Underwood waved her off. "Eh, I'll be fine. More important things to do, like get back on my Harley."

"You two know each other," Harris's hand still hanging in the air. "Wait, of course you do."

"We go way back," Cassie said. "Dr. Underwood let me bribe him with my chocolate chip cookies on more than one occasion."

Underwood shifted from foot to foot. "When she says bribe—"

Cassie patted him on the arm. "I'm sure Detective Harris is a lot more interested in what you have to say about Elizabeth's body than your sugar intake."

"Right." The breath Underwood blew out in relief ruffled his mustache. "This way."

Harris turned and quirked an eye at Cassie. "I have not seen that man smile in the two years I've known him."

"I make *really* good chocolate chip cookies," Cassie said. "He's a nice guy once you work out his quirks."

"Guess you gotta be a little weird to work here," Harris said.

Cassie gestured for Harris to go first and the two women followed in Underwood's wake as they made their way down a hall and a set of stairs. It was colder downstairs, and Cassie knew it wasn't because of the cooling units for storing bodies. The memory of an electric hum filled her fingers and toes, and she could almost feel what it was like to have her powers at full capacity. She hadn't yet decided if she liked or wanted that feeling.

"We don't have much time," Underwood said, "so I have to make this quick."

"Works for me," Cassie said. She was already chilled to the bone.

The room was larger than she remembered. She could feel the spirits crowding her. But what caught her attention was the table in the center of the room. It was covered in a sheet and there was a light shining straight down on it, illuminating the body underneath in a way that felt unnatural.

Cassie always felt like, at any moment, a body would sit up and look at her. Seeing ghosts was less terrifying than the idea that someone hadn't been dead all that time. Or they were dead, and they'd come back to life.

Not for the first time in her life, Cassie prayed zombies weren't real.

"Elizabeth Montgomery." Underwood pulled out her chart and read from it. "Twenty-eight years old. Seven-and-a-quarter-inch horizontal laceration that severed the carotid artery and damaged the windpipe. Ten-and-three-eighths-inch vertical laceration. Several broken ribs. Missing heart."

"Just like the others," Harris whispered.

"Identical other than small variations in the length of the lacerations and the damage to the chest cavity." Underwood looked up at the two women. "Are you ready?"

Harris looked at Cassie, who nodded. When she turned back to Underwood, her face was set in a mask of neutral professionalism. "Go ahead."

Underwood peeled back the sheet, stopping it above Elizabeth's hip bones. Cassie couldn't help the sharp gasp as she inhaled deeply. She had seen more than her fair share of dead bodies, but this was one of the worst.

"Can you walk me through it?" Harris asked, her voice steady.

Underwood's tone was casual, but Cassie knew him well enough to know that what he saw in his line of work stayed with him. It was a given that this case would, too.

"Toxicology shows Rohypnol in her system. She was drugged, presumably to make her easier to deal with. There are no defensive wounds which tells me she was pretty out of it when the attack started, though the pain would have flooded her system with adrenaline and snapped her back to reality, at least somewhat."

"Are you able to tell which happened first?" Cassie pointed between the woman's neck and chest.

"It looks like he cut her throat first and drained as much of her blood as possible. Her death would've been quick, all things considered. Cutting the carotid artery means she would've bled out in about a minute give or take. After that he cut out her heart."

Cassie knew there was nothing quick about it. The saving grace was upon passing through the veil to the afterlife, the pain and fear were forgotten. Usually.

Harris looked up at Underwood. "You sound like you have more to say about that."

"It's interesting." Underwood twisted the end of his mustache. "The blade cut through her neck like butter. That tells me it was sharper than steel, maybe something like obsidian."

Cassie looked over at Harris. "Are obsidian blades ever used in ritualistic killings?"

"Yes," Harris said. "What about her chest?"

"The chest was cut with the same blade," Underwood continued. "The line is steady and even, which tells me this isn't the first time the killer made an incision like this. But what's more interesting is that he used a bone saw to cut through her ribs to get to the heart."

"A bone saw?" Cassie asked. "Like what a doctor would use?"

"Exactly like what a doctor would use," Underwood said. "This guy knew what he was doing."

"Does that mean the killer is a doctor?" Cassie asked.

"Maybe," Harris said. "We don't have enough evidence to prove that yet. Hunters know plenty about anatomy, animals or otherwise, and there are ways to get your hand on any kind of tool. Is he a hunter? Did he learn it by watching YouTube and practicing on cadavers or animals?"

"But someone would hear a bone saw, wouldn't they?" Cassie asked.

"If they did," Harris said, "they might think they're hearing a chainsaw. Not a whole lot of people who run toward that sound in the middle of the woods in the middle of the night."

Cassie knew she was right. She looked back down at Elizabeth and a well of emotion filled her chest. She was sad and angry and scared and confused all at once. The poor woman had done nothing wrong other than perhaps allow the wrong man to get close to her. And here she was, spread open like a specimen for dissection. She deserved better than that. She deserved to see her thirties and beyond.

Cassie was hit with a wave of nausea when the lights flickered overhead. She looked up at Harris and Underwood, but neither of them looked alarmed. Cassie knew this was a message only for her. Between one breath and the next, Elizabeth appeared in the corner of the room.

Elizabeth walked toward Cassie with her arm outstretched, like she was pleading, begging for her life. Cassie wondered if that was the same face she made when her executioner had pulled out his knife and pressed it to her throat. The nausea in Cassie's stomach threatened to spill over.

Elizabeth dropped her arm and looked down at her body. Another tear slid down her cheek and she looked into Cassie's eyes. Anger filled the spirit's face, and she took one step toward Cassie, then another. When she was inches from Cassie, Elizabeth leaned close and whispered in Cassie's ear.

"It'll be over soon."

"Cassie, are you okay?"

Harris's voice broke the spell. The lights returned to normal, shining bright overhead. Elizabeth was gone and left in her wake was the feeling of her ghostly breath on Cassie's ear. She couldn't help but shiver. When she looked up, both the detective and Underwood were staring at her like she had grown another head.

"Yeah. I'm okay."

Harris took a step forward with a curious look in her eye. "Did you see—"

"Just dizzy." Cassie gave the detective a tight frown. "I think that might be enough for me tonight."

Underwood took the hint and covered Elizabeth's body.

"Thank you again, Dr. Underwood. We'll see ourselves out."

Harris led the way back up the stairs and down the hallway to the front entrance. They left the building and as soon as Cassie felt the fresh air on her skin, the nausea started to drift away.

"Did you see something?" Harris asked.

"Elizabeth." Cassie's tongue was dry and heavy. "She said the same thing Hannah did. *'It'll be over soon'.*"

"If he slit her throat before opening her chest, maybe he was speaking to her? Trying to reassure her?"

"Or maybe it means all of this will be over soon and our window of opportunity to catch the killer is dwindling," Cassie suggested.

"I don't like the sound of that."

"Yeah, me neither."

17

Cassie woke up on Saturday morning with a renewed vigor. Electricity buzzed through her body.

While she slept her brain had worked on Elizabeth's case, and dawn had brought with it plenty of new questions. The idea that these were ritualistic killings circled Cassie's mind. Learning that the weapon could be an obsidian knife added to that theory. And she knew where to go to prove her theory.

Dr. George Schafer volunteered at the local library. Twice a month, he lectured for free on a different artist, ranging from today's world all the way back to Ancient Greece and beyond. Cassie had attended a few times and it was such a thrill to see people young and old alike enjoying his talks. Art history wasn't always the most thrilling of subjects, but Dr. Schafer found ways to keep it engaging.

George had a way of connecting to people through art and his breadth of knowledge was astounding. With forty years of experience under his belt, he knew a little about a lot. And when he didn't know the answer, he took the time to look it up and get back to you. He was a bit of a local hero for those who knew him.

Today's lecture was on one of Cassie's favorite artists—Artemisia Gentileschi. She was a seventeenth-century Italian painter who rose above her station as a woman to make a name for herself. She often painted women from myth and figures from the Bible. Artemisia's rape played a pivotal role in her art, and Cassie had always been taken aback by the power depicted in her paintings, particularly *Judith Slaying Holofernes*.

Looking at it projected on the overhead screen that hung from the library's wall, Cassie was overcome with emotion. She felt a kinship with the artist who lived with unspeakable pain and yet found a way to channel her anger and bravery into her work. She didn't let society's rules dictate who she should be. She instead used every opportunity to defy expectations and prove she was as good—if not better—than her male peers.

Cassie waited until the room cleared, and she approached George, who was packing his equipment. One of the library staff wheeled the projector away, and when George noticed Cassie's presence, a grin broke out across his face.

"Ms. Quinn! What a pleasant surprise. How'd I do?"

"Incredible, as always." Cassie found it easy to compliment George. He was a kind soul who gave his time for free. "She's one of my favorites."

"I seem to remember that from your entry interview." George winked at her and grew serious. "How are you?"

"Been having some trouble sleeping," Cassie said, "but I'm feeling good today."

"That's fantastic to hear." George paused and stared at

Cassie, trying to read her mind. "You didn't come here on a whim."

"You're right."

"Should we grab a chair?"

Cassie nodded and followed George into an alcove where they could talk in private. The library had set up a temporary display full of female authors and artists to coincide with the lecture. Cassie was delighted to see young girls each picking out several books to read.

"So, Ms. Quinn, what can I do for you today?"

Cassie turned back to George and felt the color rise in her cheeks. "It's a bit unorthodox."

"I love unorthodox." He leaned back in his seat. "Hit me."

"I'm doing some research on my own, outside of work, and I'm stuck. I guess I was hoping you might be able to point me in the right direction?"

"I can do my best. What are you researching?"

Cassie braced herself. "Ritualistic sacrifice?"

George's eyes sparkled and for a moment Cassie considered the idea that he saw through her farce and knew why she was asking him for help. "A fascinating subject."

"Is it?"

"It's part of why we enjoy Ms. Gentileschi's work, isn't it? Often violent and gruesome, but there's a strange catharsis there. Art, whether it's a painting or a book or a movie, is designed to tell us a story. We can relate to it in a myriad of ways. Art can invite us to join in on a celebration or it could warn us against danger. Old wives' tales, for example, are an oral tradition that stem from real-life horrors. Urban legends might make us pause before we step out into the middle of the night for an evening stroll. Ritualistic sacrifice has been around for millennia. It's nothing to glorify, but we as a global community continue to be fascinated by it. I think that's human nature."

"That makes me feel a little better," Cassie admitted.

George smiled. "So, are we talking about human sacrifice according to the Aztec empire, or were you shooting for something more modern?"

Cassie felt sheepish. "I'm not sure. I feel like it could all apply."

George was excited. "That's true. One lays the foundation for the other. Did you know that it wasn't until recently we discovered the Spanish accounts of Aztec sacrifice were true? Apparently, they would cut open the chests of their victims and offer their still-beating hearts to the gods. Sometimes they would consume parts of their bodies to be closer with their deities."

"But why?" She knew this was the question entire groups of scholars spent lifetimes trying to answer. She decided to narrow it down. "What did their hearts symbolize?"

"The Aztecs considered the heart to be the seat of an individual, an important part of their personhood. Liberating this part and giving it to the gods was a great honor."

"So, the sacrifices were voluntary?"

"Not always. It depended on the objective. Was a person offering themselves in sacrifice to a deity, or was someone sacrificing another person to *their* deity? It sounds like splitting hairs, but you can imagine the difference is extreme when you're sitting at the sharp end of the knife."

Cassie couldn't argue with that. She was sure the three women killed over the last few weeks would agree. But Cassie couldn't say for certain they had been ritualistically sacrificed.

The detectives hadn't found the hearts which was more significant than not.

"So," Cassie wondered how long it would take George to catch on. "How has this ritualistic sacrifice transformed over the years?"

George leaned back in his chair and steepled his fingers. "Different cultures have used human sacrifice for different reasons all throughout history. As you can imagine, modern society frowns upon such practices."

"But it does still happen."

"There are cults around the world that still believe in the power of human sacrifice." George gave Cassie a significant look. "Many serial killers also conduct such a practice."

"I'm not being as clever as I think, am I?"

"No, you're not." He tapped the side of his nose. "But, to your credit, I wouldn't have connected the dots if it hadn't been for your visitor the other day."

Cassie hung her head. "Detective Harris. I'm sorry about that—"

He held up a hand. "There's no need to apologize. You're not in any trouble, are you?"

"No. She wanted to know if I had any insight into the killings given my prior, ah, experience." George did not know about Cassie's ability to see spirits, but he was aware of her connection to Novak. "I told her I didn't know of anything that could help, but I haven't been able to get the case out of my head since."

George nodded sagely. "It is not always clear why serial killers act the way they do. I am by no means an expert here, although I don't think it takes a genius to see that each person, each killer, has their own motive and ways of coping with trauma."

"So, if a person were to, say, cut out someone's heart and drain all their blood, what do you think their motive and trauma would be?"

George laughed. "I think that's a question better suited for the police. But, if we're considering this an act of ritualistic sacrifice, it could have several different meanings. A lot of cultures place great emphasis on certain organs as well as a person's blood. The heart, for instance, is what keeps us alive, but it also represents love. People can die from a broken heart. The Aztecs also knew of its power, which is why they offered it to their gods. Its removal, I would imagine, could either represent a freeing of the victim's personhood or love, or a punishment for those same two principles."

"And the blood?" Cassie asked.

George looked at her for a few seconds. "The papers haven't mentioned anything about the way the victims have been killed."

Cassie looked around to make sure they were alone. "That may be insider information."

"In that case, I will keep it to myself." George leaned forward. "Blood also gives us life by carrying oxygen to our cells. Some consider it to have healing properties. Bloodletting was the act of withdrawing blood from a patient to prevent or cure an illness. We know diseases don't work that way. On the other hand, there's a reason why blood sacrifices are often made to gods and demons. We still believe there's a lot of power in our blood."

Cassie shook her head. "It's weird to think people still believe in that."

George shrugged. "People who take communion are consuming the body and blood of Christ, are they not?"

"Yeah," Cassie said, "but that's metaphorical."

"Is it that much of a stretch? I don't condone such practices, but ritualistic sacrifice, to me, would seem less crazy if I were truly desperate. Imagine that all your crops are dying, and a shaman tells you that if you cut off the head of your neighbor and bury it in your field, your crops will begin to grow. Most people wouldn't jump straight to murder but imagine that your family is starving to death. Can't you imagine you'd try anything if you thought you could get away with it?"

"Yeah, but that stuff doesn't work," Cassie said.

"Maybe not. But that's not the point, is it? It provides hope and sometimes that can be more promising than anything reality provides."

It still seemed like a strange idea, especially here in Savannah, but then again, she could talk to ghosts. Who was she to say what was real and what was not?

"Are the police considering ritualistic sacrifice?" George asked.

"I'm not sure. In all honesty, I don't think they know what to do with the information they have. They're looking into anything that might explain why someone would do this to those women."

George nodded solemnly. "What happened to those women was a terrible crime." He eyed Cassie and measured his words with caution. "But it's not your responsibility to solve this case."

Cassie's mouth tightened. What could she say to that? In a way, he was right. But knowing what those women went through made her heart ache. Survivor's guilt, they call it. She felt bad for being alive while the three women wound up dead.

Cassie knew she couldn't have stopped their deaths and yet, her brain was yelling at her to do something, anything, so it didn't happen to another person.

Plus, there was Elizabeth. Somewhere along life's path, Cassie decided that if she had the ability to fix a terrible injustice, it was her responsibility to do that. She wasn't some girl who considered herself an amateur detective. She could communicate with the dead and that gave her a leg up on most people, including the police department.

"I know." Cassie tried to put some weight behind her words. "But helping feels better than doing nothing."

George looked proud. "You're a good person, Ms. Quinn. We need more people like you in this world."

"I don't know about that." She wouldn't wish her abilities on anyone. "But that means a lot coming from you."

18

Cassie emerged from the Bull Street Library to four missed calls from Harris. She stopped dead in her tracks with a heart so heavy it sunk to her toes. When Cassie called the detective back, her worst fears were realized. Harris did not mince her words.

"Another woman has been killed."

Cassie stopped dead in her tracks. "Are you serious?"

"Just like the others." Detective Harris took a deep breath. "I know I have no right to ask—"

"I'll be right there."

Cassie got the address from Harris and hopped in her car without thought. Halfway there, Cassie understood what she was feeling.

Guilt.

She should've been able to do more. She should've listened to Elizabeth sooner. She should've tried harder. If she had, maybe this latest victim wouldn't have fallen prey to this killer.

Maybe he would already be in prison and Cassie would be moving on with her life.

When Cassie arrived at the crime scene, a few vehicles were parked nearby. A couple of people stood off to one side and several police cars were blocking the park's entrance.

Cassie pulled up and gave them her name. She was waved right through.

By the time she parked and got out of her vehicle, Harris was there to meet her. She looked tired, like she hadn't slept much last night. Her ponytail wasn't as sleek and smooth as normal, and dark circles had formed under her eyes.

"Are you ready for this?" Harris asked.

"No," Cassie said. "But let's go."

"Her name is Sage Washington. Black female. Twenty-six. Throat slit and heart removed. She was found about an hour ago by some park goers who were foraging and came across her body. I got here about half an hour ago."

"You sound rushed."

Harris looked around. "We're trying to keep the media away. That's why we've set the perimeter back so far. We don't want anyone to know how the women were killed in case we can use it against any suspects."

"Makes sense." Cassie felt a knot form in her stomach. "And what are you expecting of me here?"

Harris took a moment to answer. They stepped off the path and made their way deeper into the woods. It wasn't hard to figure out where they had to go. There was a circle of cops standing amidst the trees, and inside that, a circle of yellow caution tape. As they passed by, every one of the cops nodded in acknowledgement to Harris. No one wanted her job that morning. Or most mornings, Cassie imagined.

"Detective Klein said fresh crime scenes can leave a bigger imprint for you to pick up." Harris formed the words like she was repeating what David told her without knowing what he meant. "I don't like to bring civilians to a crime scene like this but you're not the typical civilian."

"I'm choosing to take that as a compliment."

Harris halted outside the crime scene tape and looked back at Cassie. "I know you already saw Elizabeth's body, but it's always worse outside of a medical facility. If you think you're going to get sick—"

"I'll walk away," Cassie said. "I know the drill."

Harris nodded her head once and lifted the tape so they both could pass under it. Cassie could see the body up ahead, but she searched the woods around the area first.

Nothing seemed out of the ordinary. Like Hannah's dumping site, this one seemed to have been chosen arbitrarily. It didn't look anything like the other one. The trees weren't the same, nothing had been erected as a warning or a tribute and, all things considered, nothing seemed out of place.

Cassie could see the body out of the corner of her eye and her stomach turned. She wasn't prone to queasiness these days, given all she had already seen, but there was something terrible and unnatural about being able to peer inside someone's rib cage. She could've gone her entire life without experiencing that.

But as Harris led her closer to the body, Cassie felt drawn to it, and when they were close enough to see the entire picture, she couldn't look away.

Sage's face was pale and lifeless. Her eyes were still open, staring unceasingly at the sky above. Her throat had been sliced in the same way Elizabeth's had, at least according to Cassie's untrained eyes. The front of her navy dress was covered in blood, but not as much as Cassie would've expected. If the killer was collecting the blood as it drained, though, that made sense.

What Cassie couldn't get past was the woman's open chest. It was a bloody mess, far worse than what she had seen with Elizabeth. The rib cage had been cut and spread open in the same way, but blood and leaves blown around by the wind made it look more congested.

"How long do you think she's been here?" Cassie asked.

"We know he kills in the middle of the night and leaves the body to be found the next morning. It's, what, almost eleven? I'd say between eight and ten hours."

"Do we know anything about her yet?" Cassie asked. "Anything significant?"

"We're still running a background check. Trying to find her next of kin." Harris blew out a breath. "God, I hate this part."

"It's not your fault." Cassie wondered if she was trying to convince Harris or herself of that truth. "There's not enough evidence to find the killer yet. There's nothing you could've done to stop this."

"Yeah, well..." Harris broke off and shook her head.

Cassie could feel the punch coming. "You can say what you need to."

"It's nothing. I'm just frustrated. And I never thought I'd be the type of cop to put stock in a psychic."

"Especially one that's not getting results?"

"I didn't say that."

"You didn't have to. It's not like I'm not aware I've been less than helpful."

Harris didn't respond and Cassie returned her gaze to the

body. It was better than standing in whatever angry silence was emanating off the detective.

Cassie backed up a few feet and started doing a wide circle around the crime scene. Harris followed behind, presumably to make sure she didn't trample on any potential evidence. Cassie was grateful for the reprieve from the conversation, though she could still feel Harris's frustration in the air.

Cassie noticed the air around her was already warm and humid, and the breeze didn't do much to quell the heat. She felt comfortable as she always did in the summer but noticed many of the cops sweating underneath their uniforms.

What Cassie couldn't feel was that same hint of electric buzz that she had felt at the city morgue where she had anticipated Elizabeth's presence and almost felt like her old self. The one who had been able to tap into her abilities and offer guidance on a case.

What did she do in the past? Close her eyes and feel for the other world? No. The other world came to her, uninvited and unrelenting. She spent a decade trying to control it, trying to lead a normal life, and here she was unable to tap back into it. What was holding her back?

It couldn't be because Novak was gone. The little boy's spirit and Elizabeth's initial visit disproved that. Her powers had faded, but they hadn't gone away.

And as she embroiled herself further into this case, she could feel her gift wanting to come back. The buzzing of electricity was under the surface. She could feel it wanting to reach out and grab onto her.

But then she thought of work. And that made her think of Jason. And her family.

Could she live a normal life with these abilities? She had

spent a long time alone because of them. Would she be able to hide them if she had a social life, a love life? Would she want to? And if she didn't, what would the people around her think? Would they think she was crazy, or would they embrace her abilities? Would they try to take advantage of them?

"Are you getting anything?" Harris hissed.

Cassie was yanked from her thoughts. The questions filling her mind were not ideal for keeping a clear head. She turned to Harris. "No, I'm sorry."

Harris was saved from offering empty reassurances when a pudgy, balding officer walked up to them. He looked between Cassie and Harris but must've dismissed any questions he had.

"The media's here," he told Harris. "*She's* here."

"Shit."

19

As soon as Harris and Cassie made their way back to the trail, Cassie didn't have to wonder who *"she"* was. Cassie spotted the blonde reporter she had seen on the news channel the other day. Her curls were as bright and bouncy as ever, and the look on her face was one of triumph. The reporter knew Harris didn't want her there, and she didn't care.

Harris turned back to the pudgy man. "I don't want anyone near that crime scene who doesn't belong. The media gets nothing. Not even a grainy image of her body, got it?"

But Cassie wasn't paying attention to their exchange. She watched as one of the guards left his post and walked right up to the reporter. He tossed a look over his shoulder before leaning in close to her and whispering something. Cassie couldn't hear what they were saying, but by the look on the woman's face, she was trying to turn on her charm. It wasn't working, and the man pointed a finger at her and walked away.

He returned to his post and looked back at Harris, catching Cassie's eye in the process.

"What are you going to say to her?" the pudgy man asked as Cassie tuned back into their conversation.

"Whatever I need to," Harris said.

Cassie didn't know what to do. She didn't want to leave in case Harris still needed her, but she also didn't want to be caught on camera. Chances are she already was, but she could be mistaken for another detective.

Still, Cassie inched her way to the barrier where a few more stragglers looked on. Most of them had the decency to keep their phones away, but for the ones who didn't, Cassie offered her back.

Harris's voice wasn't difficult to hear. "Ms. Campbell. Always a pleasure."

"Is it, Detective?" The reporter's southern twang was in full effect this morning. "I get the distinct impression you don't want to talk to me."

"It's not personal." Harris kept her tone professional. "I'm trying to do a job, Ms. Campbell, and when I'm distracted by the media, I have trouble doing that job."

"The people have a right to know whether or not there's a serial killer on the loose in Savannah."

"As I explained the other day, I cannot release details of an open investigation. We must uphold the integrity of the case to ensure there is no misinformation."

"Do you think there's a significance that all the women who've been killed have had their hearts ripped out of their chest? What do you think that means?"

Harris looked like the reporter had sucker punched her. She recovered but had revealed that Ms. Campbell had perhaps hit too close to home. "Like I said, I can't comment on an open investigation. Once I'm able to release any details, I'll be sure to contact one of the other news channels."

Cassie had the distinct pleasure of seeing a flash of anger cross the reporter's face. Harris turned around and stalked toward Cassie. The detective grabbed Cassie's elbow and steered her further away from the growing crowd.

"Have you told anyone the details I shared with you about the investigation?"

Cassie opened her mouth to say no. She hadn't, but she remembered the conversation she had had with George earlier that morning.

Harris must've caught the look on her face. "You've got to be kidding me."

"I trust him with my life," Cassie said. "He would never—"

"The media got wind of it somehow, so it doesn't matter how much you trust him."

"That's impossible."

Harris hooked a thumb over her shoulder. "The news says otherwise."

"I told him this morning, right before you called me. There's no way he could've told anyone." Cassie's brain was frantic. "Plus, she already knew something the other day when you were on the news."

The silence stretched on.

"I'm really sorry—" Cassie started.

Harris held up a hand. She waited for a beat. "I can't stress enough how important it is that the information I divulge to you is in strict confidence. Ms. Campbell is getting her information from somewhere else, but that is no excuse for you to go around prattling about the case to whomever you feel like discussing it with."

"I wasn't *prattling*." Cassie couldn't keep the hurt out of her voice. "Dr. George Schafer is my boss at the museum. He's an academic and a respected member of the community. I trust him with sensitive information."

"To be frank, Ms. Quinn, this sensitive information isn't for you to share."

"You trusted me enough to be a part of this investigation in whatever capacity I could. I went to Dr. Schafer because I thought he might have pertinent information."

"And?" Harris asked. "Did he?"

"So, you *do* want to hear it? Or do you want to yell at me some more?"

Harris leaned in close. "Ms. Quinn, I have four dead bodies on my hands and a plucky reporter halfway up my ass. I don't need your sarcasm. I need your help."

Cassie took a deep breath to calm her anger. "I may have come across something that could back up your theory about the occult."

"I'm listening."

"I went to George asking about ritualistic sacrifice throughout history. There are a lot of reasons why someone might perform a human sacrifice. They may want to honor a god or placate a demon. They could want to heal their land or another person. The rituals involve the heart or blood and their actions have meaning. There's symbolism to the sacrifice."

The detective looked at Cassie and, not for the first time, Cassie felt like she was being sized up. "What I'm about to share with you stays between us. Is that understood?"

Cassie stopped herself from rolling her eyes. "Yes. Of course."

"Underwood called me this morning. There's been a discrepancy."

"What kind of discrepancy?"

"Elizabeth's medical charts say her blood type was A Positive, but she had a Red Cross donation card in her wallet at the time of death. It says she's O negative."

"That's a big mistake to make in someone's medical records."

"That's the thing. I don't think it was a mistake." Harris's eyes had a fire in them. "I think her records were changed. Everything is digital these days. If you have the right equipment, time, and knowledge, it can be done."

"You think the murderer hacked Elizabeth's medical records?"

"I'm not coming to any conclusions yet." Harris crossed her arms and lowered her voice. "But it's the killer's first real mistake. And our first real lead. There could be a digital trace. And given that Underwood was insistent that the killer knew what he was doing when he opened the victim's chest, I can see this leading back to a hospital. But there's still a lot to work through."

"I suppose that could make sense," Cassie said.

"You don't sound convinced."

"No, I just don't like the idea that this could be a doctor or a nurse."

"Wouldn't be the first time," Harris said. "There's a whole category for it: Angel of Death."

"But those are mercy killings. This doesn't feel like mercy to me."

"What about *it'll be over soon?*" Harris asked. "That could fit in with the idea of a mercy killing."

Cassie looked around and lowered her voice. "Their hearts were ripped out of their chests. What would be the purpose of that?"

Harris tipped her head back. "I don't know."

Cassie let the silence hang in the air for thirty seconds. "What are we going to do?"

"You're going to go home and wait until I call you. I don't want you investigating any more crime scenes or confiding in any more associates."

"Please, I can help—"

"Ms. Quinn, do I need to remind you that you are not a detective, nor are you a police officer?"

"No, of course not. I—"

"Do I need to remind you that you are not an official consultant on this case?"

"No. Please, detective—"

"I appreciate your insight into the case, and I will take your advice about ritualistic sacrifices into consideration." Harris walked Cassie back over to the barricade keeping the public back. "For now, I have a stronger, more promising lead to follow regarding the doctor angle. If that leads to a dead end, you will be the first person I call. Until then, please give me room to do my job."

"Of course." Cassie was angry at the way her voice trembled. "I'm sorry for any inconvenience I've caused."

Harris looked down at her watch. When she spoke, her voice was still cool. "It's been no inconvenience at all."

Cassie knew it was a lie.

20

He muted the TV and slammed the remote down on the table in the middle of the living room. Part of him wanted to cringe—it was an antique, after all—and another part of him wished to throw it through the window instead.

He did neither.

He stood and paced the room. The police force was doing a shoddy job of keeping the murders quiet. That lead detective, Harris, cared little for the young reporter with the blonde curls revealing more information than she should.

The reporter aggravated him, too.

To expect that his entire operation could fly under the radar would have been naïve. He knew that he'd receive some media attention, but he had hoped it'd be another week or two before that happened. Speeding up his timeline wasn't appealing, but something needed to change.

He had thought about taking the correspondent as his next victim, or even the detective, but neither one of them fulfilled his needs. Plus, that would bring more attention to his operation. It would have been easier to kill the reporter, and maybe more satisfying given her smug appearance, but there was no way he could justify it.

He wasn't a monster.

He had a job to do.

But he was also a realist. He wouldn't take the option off the table, not completely. As a last resort, one of the women may have to go. Perhaps one could be used as a red herring of sorts. It could throw the cops and media off his trail and make them second guess what they thought they knew about the case.

The idea sparked his imagination and he chastised himself for not thinking of this sooner. Anger welled inside of him and he had to flee. He had to be outside. He had to be anywhere but here.

Through the hall, out the door, and down the front steps. The sun was warm on his face and had an immediate calming effect. It renewed his sense of purpose. He never wanted to lose this feeling. Taking stock of the fourth marker in his yard, he noted how the empty hole seemed to pull him. Last night he had retrieved the necessary ingredients to enact the next part of the ritual, but he had needed to wait one more day to put it in its proper place.

The sun dimmed with a passing cloud in time with his darkening mood. These were the hardest days. He had everything required, but he had to be patient. Forever patient.

The reporter was a problem. The detective, too. These problems would have to wait. He was several steps ahead of them. Neither woman had a clue as to his true motive, and if they figured it out—as unlikely as it was—he had the perfect wrench to throw in their little machine. An unbreakable patsy to make sure he remained untouchable.

That thought brought a smile to his face. He made his way back to his house, climbed the stairs, and returned to the living room.

This time, when he caught sight of the news, he felt no annoyance. It was in his best interest to be patient, and that's what he planned to do.

21

Cassie didn't bother figuring out where she wanted to go when she pulled away from the park. She picked a direction and floored it.

Anger bubbled inside of her like a volcano, but she didn't know why. Yes, Harris had dismissed her, but the detective hadn't raised her voice or insulted her. She also hadn't lied. Cassie was not working on the case in any official capacity. Besides, her theories were also just that—theories. Cassie had no evidence and no solid reason to force Harris to investigate the occult theory instead of the doctor theory.

Cassie learned a long time ago that being a detective was not like in the movies. Detectives in the real world are lucky to have their first or second or even third lead pan out. One clue didn't always lead to the next right away. It was a lot of leg work and a lot of dead ends. A lot of wasted time to get to the correct answer. A lot of dead bodies.

So, why was she still fuming?

Cassie took one deep breath and then another. She knew she wasn't frustrated with the detective or the case. She was frustrated with herself. She was mad about getting involved again, mad about caring. She couldn't turn that part of herself off and she didn't want to, but empathy was sometimes exhausting.

She wanted this, but what would it cost? She had waited so long to get a job that satisfied her. A couple months in, she was already taking a day off to do some extracurricular detective work. She had put off going out with a guy she liked because she was too busy trying to figure out how to solve Elizabeth's case.

And when this case is resolved, would that be the end? What about the little boy who disappeared? What about the next ghost to stroll into her life, demanding her full attention? Savannah was full of dead bodies, old and new. Every step she took in the city was on a path of bones and she was always in danger of stumbling over the next one. Was that the future she wanted for herself?

With her anger slipping away, Cassie took stock of her surroundings. But her heart pounded harder, threatening to leap out of her chest and onto the road in front of her. She was familiar with this part of Savannah. For the rest of her life, she would never forget what happened to her here.

Rather than driving on, Cassie quelled her shaking hands and pulled into Bonaventure Cemetery's entrance. Sweat formed on her brow that had nothing to do with the heat, but she pushed away the fear as she acknowledged it. This place and the man who tried to end her life here no longer had a hold on her.

Cassie parked her car and took a moment to collect herself.

Once she did, she stepped out of the vehicle, picked a direction, and started walking.

It was not the first time she had been back to this place and she doubted it would be the last. Her therapist had encouraged her to visit it once she felt ready. It's where Cassie learned all about exposure therapy. The first time, she couldn't get out of the car. The second time, she had passed out before taking two steps.

But every time she tried, she got farther.

Now, Cassie could walk the entire cemetery. It wasn't comfortable by any means, but it was tolerable. That was a huge win in her book, though she felt she had a long way to go. It might be ten more years until this place didn't have any effect on her. Or maybe it always would. She had come to terms with that a long time ago.

Once Cassie got over her initial fear, she came to respect this place. She felt closer to the spirit world here. Whether because this was where it all started or because there were more spirits here, she was not sure. When the anxiety had become less intense and more controllable, she had realized the cemetery made her feel stronger.

She could feel that electric buzz that had been missing in the museum. The one that started to take form in the city morgue.

It was a tingling sensation that ran the length of her body, sometimes gathering in her toes, her fingertips, the top of her head. She was like a conduit and her limbs were the points of entry for her abilities. Despite her years of living with these sensations, she still didn't know what caused them. David had plenty of theories, but Cassie didn't take stock in those.

They existed and that was all that mattered.

Cassie found a stone bench along one of the paths and sat

down. The warmth of the rock seeped into her body, a pleasant mix with the electricity. She couldn't say she was happy, but there was something affirming in the sensation. The void evaporated, replaced with a power that made her strong and capable and unique.

It surprised her to realize how much she had missed it.

To others, she looked ordinary. Maybe she was there to visit the grave of a friend or loved one. Maybe she was meeting someone to offer them moral support. Maybe she was grieving the loss in her own way. But she was so much more.

It was a beautiful Saturday afternoon, and many people were paying their respects to the dead. A few groups here and there, but mostly people in ones and twos visiting graves and laying flowers down. In between each grave, the spirits roamed. Some were fainter than others, but their glitching, almost translucent look was the biggest clue that they no longer walked the earth.

They didn't pay much attention to Cassie. It was a relief when she first started visiting the cemetery. Her greatest fear was being inundated with spirits seeking her help, following her home and begging her to pass on messages.

But most of the spirits here were waiting for their loved ones to visit before moving on. A few would stand alone forever, but most wanted that final goodbye. They only had eyes for their friends, families, and lovers.

When the ghosts did notice Cassie, not all of them were brave or strong enough to communicate with her. Not all of them needed her help. She always wondered what they could feel from her, how they learned she could help them move on. Was it something they just knew, deep in their souls?

She thought back to Elizabeth. Something had drawn the

woman to Cassie's house, to her bedroom, in the middle of the night. Something told her where to go, where to ask for help. But asking *why* and *how* was a dangerous game. In over ten years, Cassie hadn't learned the answers to those questions and so decided to stop asking them.

Besides, there were other questions she could answer. Unlike most of the ghosts in the graveyard, Elizabeth had been ruthlessly murdered. Her story needed to be told, and her mystery deserved to be solved.

Cassie felt her anger flair up once more. She got to her feet and continued her circuit around the cemetery, taking in the names and dates on the various headstones. She forced herself to let go of the events from the last few days and enjoy the warmth of the sun and the calm of the graveyard.

A few minutes later, she found herself standing at the foot of a recent grave. It was covered in fresh flowers and wreaths. Along the top of the headstone, Cassie caught sight of piles of coins and little stones. Notes had been folded in half and placed under a few of the rocks.

She put two and two together. This was the gravesite of one of the victims of the recent string of murders.

Cassie looked up and down the pathway, wondering if anyone else was on their way to pay respects to the woman. She hadn't yet decided what she was going to do, but she didn't want anyone to see her do it.

She doubled down on that notion as soon as she turned back around and saw a young woman crouched over the grave with her head in her hands.

22

The young woman appeared as though she had been sitting there all along. Her jet-black hair looked faded and lifeless. Her skin was translucent, but she didn't glitch out as often as Elizabeth had. She looked more corporeal. Almost alive.

Until she looked up.

Cassie took an involuntary step back. The quiet hum of electricity circulating through her body was sharp and painful. The top of her head felt warm and the tips of her fingers went numb. The ghost's gaze bore into her, as though searching her mind for answers. Cassie couldn't help but break the connection, choosing instead to look down at the headstone.

Her name was Jessica Tran.

Cassie returned her gaze to the woman and gasped upon seeing her standing. She still looked at Cassie with intense eyes, but with less fire. Perhaps she found what she was looking for.

She wore a plain navy dress. Her hair hung down to her waist and the ends fluttered in an otherworldly breeze. There was a ghastly mark across her neck. Her chest had been opened and her heart removed. Blood soaked into the material, leaving splotches of wet cloth to glisten in the sun.

Cassie could feel the strength of this woman. Her anger fueled her ability to stay connected to earth's realm. She had been dead longer than Elizabeth, so she had had more time to understand what was happening to her. She would be able to control her spirit form better than Elizabeth, too.

When Jessica stepped closer and spoke, it was with a clear voice that didn't struggle to escape her throat.

"It'll be over soon."

Cassie's heart stopped. It was the same line Hannah and Elizabeth had given her.

"I don't understand," Cassie said. "I don't know what that means."

"It'll be over soon," Jessica repeated. There was a flash of anger in her eyes.

"I'm sorry, I—"

Jessica took another step forward and pressed her hand against Cassie's cheek. It felt like the memory of a touch. It was cool and light, but Cassie only had a second or two to comprehend the feeling when an image sliced its way into her brain.

Cassie stood inside an open structure. There was a roof over her head, but she could feel the breeze blowing by her, carrying the muffled sound of cars and music and voices and laughter and the smell of the river and the restaurants. She felt dizzy and drunk, too tired to stand on her own but unsure of where to go or what to do.

There was a scraping noise and she looked up. In front of her, there was a white vehicle with a large green sticker on the side that read *Savannah Non-Emergency Medical Transport Van*. A man with his back to her was opening the side doors. He was tall and well-built with brown hair. He was wearing dress pants and a collared shirt, but she couldn't see his face.

Cassie swayed on her feet and looked in the direction of the breeze. Although she couldn't see the street, she realized she was several stories off the ground. It was nighttime and the moon hung low in the sky. She could barely make out whooping and yelling from below.

A touch at her elbow alarmed Cassie. She turned back around and realized the man had left the van and was by her side, guiding her toward the vehicle. Something felt off, but in her confusion, she didn't know what to do. As the car got closer to her, her vision started to fade.

In a panic, Cassie tried to look over at the man next to her, but her vision faded, and she was back in the cemetery.

She blinked against the bright Georgia sun, staring in the face of an elderly woman who had her hand on Cassie's elbow.

"Are you okay?" the woman asked.

Cassie didn't know how to answer. She was still unsteady on her feet and she couldn't remember where she was or what she was doing there. When she turned back to Jessica's grave, the memory of the woman's ghost came back to her, but she was nowhere to be seen.

"Sweetheart?" the woman said. "Are you okay? Do we need to call someone?"

Cassie processed the woman in front of her. She was wearing a wide-brimmed hat and large sunglasses. A man, presumably her husband, stood behind her, shading his eyes from the sun.

"I'm okay," Cassie said. Her mouth was dry and her tongue heavy like a ten-pound weight, but her senses came flooding back. She felt steadier on her feet. "Thank you."

"The sun is brutal this time of day," the woman said. "You should wear a hat, dear."

Cassie forced a smile. "You're right. I'll go sit in my car for a minute. Cool down in the AC."

The gentleman looked down at the gravestone covered in flowers and trinkets. "Did you know her?"

"Dear," the woman chastised. "Don't be nosy."

"We were acquaintances." Cassie said. She was surprised when it didn't feel like she was lying but being inside another person's head to witness their last moments of life had a bonding effect.

"Tragic," the man shook his head. "Everyone deserves to live as long as we have."

His wife, satisfied that Cassie wasn't about to pass out, let go of her and patted her husband on the arm. "Even short lives can burn bright."

He looked up at Cassie as though pulled from his reverie. "You look a bit pale, kiddo."

"That's my natural state." She smiled again, and this one felt more natural. "Thank you again. I hope you have a good day."

"You too, dear," the woman said. "Drink some water."

Cassie waved her acknowledgement and, taking a second to make sure her feet were steady enough, walked back down the path toward her car. She felt like she had been hit by a truck and spun around until she didn't know which way was up.

She had experienced visions in the form of flashes or insane dreams she had to decipher. This one was clear, if not brief. It lasted maybe ten seconds, but the images were burned inside her brain. Jessica had spent a great amount of energy ensuring Cassie saw the medical transport van and the parking garage.

If only she had been able to see the man, too. She saw he was average height with brown hair. He wore nice clothes. Added together that could describe half the men in Savannah on any given night.

The van was a different story altogether. She hadn't seen a company logo on the van, but the green sticker was enough to go on. Maybe there was credence to Harris's doctor theory. It still didn't give them the *why*, but it did point them in the right direction as to the *who*.

But finding the van would be another story. She knew it was, at least at one point in time, parked in a garage several floors up. The sounds made her think it was in the downtown Savannah area, and though that spanned several blocks, it gave her a place to start.

Jessica had spoken the same words as Hannah, too. Cassie still didn't know what they meant, but now more than ever she felt like time was ticking away. Four women had been killed, including the latest victim, Sage Washington. If this was a ritualistic killing, their killer needed their hearts and blood for a purpose. Once he fulfilled that purpose, would he keep killing, or would he be gone forever and fade back into society like a normal person?

Cassie couldn't let that happen, even if Detective Harris wanted to keep her out of the way. The women she connected with deserved to be laid to rest, and the women of Savannah— herself included—deserved to go outside without fear that they would be the next victim.

Cassie had made up her mind before she got back to her car. She wasn't going to let Detective Harris's warning stop her from doing her own investigation.

She wanted answers.

And there was only one way to get them.

23

Detective Harris sat in her car and aimed the AC vents at her face. She took a deep breath and held it. The Georgia heat still gripped her lungs. She'd lived in Savannah for six years, but doubted she'd ever get used to the summers. Growing up in Montana made her resilient to thin air, bitter winters, and several feet of snow over the course of just a few hours. But heat and humidity together? Forget it.

She didn't regret leaving Missoula behind, even if she did miss her parents. It took some time to get used to the pace of the South, but the people were kind, and she was proud to serve the Savannah community.

But days like today were the most difficult. Putting her car in reverse, Harris backed out of the precinct parking lot and drove to the east side, searching until she found the address she was looking for. Sage Washington's house, where she had lived with her mother and two younger brothers.

Not one to delay the inevitable, Harris got out of her car,

walked up to the front of the house, pulled the screen door open and knocked on the front door. She took a step back and let the screen door fall shut. It was silent inside, but after about thirty seconds, a bolt slid back, and the door opened enough for the security chain to be drawn taut.

A young man of about fifteen peered at her from the crack. He stayed silent.

"Hi there, my name is Detective Adelaide Harris. I'm looking for your mother, Mrs. Washington? I spoke with her on the phone earlier."

The boy closed the door in her face, and for a second, Harris thought the boy had ignored her. But when the sound of the scraping chain came from inside and the door opened once more, she breathed a sigh of relief.

"Mama's in the living room," the boy said.

Harris considered that her formal invitation. She pulled open the screen door and stepped inside the tiny kitchen. It smelled like roast beef and mashed potatoes, and the savory scent reminded her she had yet to eat that day. But the thought of what came next was enough to make her forget her hunger.

The boy led Harris around a corner and into the living room. It was neat and tidy and stuffy and warm. The house didn't seem to have any air conditioning, and it was late enough in the day that keeping the windows closed would be more practical than letting the heat in just for what little breeze might make its way through the rooms.

A plump woman sat on the couch fanning herself. A cane rested against her leg, and there was a wrap around her knee, partially visible just below the hem of her dress. Another boy sat next to her in a tank top and shorts. He was younger than the first boy, maybe twelve. He stared at cartoons on the TV.

When Harris walked in, the woman looked up. Her expression was unreadable.

"Mrs. Washington?"

"Yes." Her voice was deep and even. "You're that detective then?"

"Detective Harris, ma'am."

Mrs. Washington didn't break eye contact for a long moment. Harris felt like she was being scrutinized, but she expected nothing less. This woman's daughter had just been murdered, and she knew they didn't have any current leads. Would she cooperate, or would she send Harris packing?

"Boys, go to your room."

"But mama—" the young boy said.

"Don't you talk back to me." Mrs. Washington passed her icy stare from Harris to her son. "Don't come out until I tell you to."

"Mama, can I—"

"Both of you," she said. "You don't need to hear none of this. Go."

There was no arguing, and both boys seemed to understand that. The older one switched off the TV as they made their way to the back of the house. Harris waited until she heard a door click shut before she turned back to the woman in front of her.

"Mrs. Washington, I'm so—"

"If you're about to tell me you're sorry, you can turn right back around and leave." The woman's eyes were hard. "I don't need your apologies, Detective Harris. I need answers."

"Of course." Harris gestured to an open chair. "May I?"

After a moment's hesitation, the woman nodded and then shifted in her seat, giving Harris her full attention. She waited for the detective to make the first move.

Harris sighed. She didn't know where to start. These things were never easy, and there was no single right way to do this. Some people wanted to be eased into the conversation, while others wanted to know every detail of how their loved one had died. Each person mourned in their own way.

"I'm here to ask you a few questions about your daughter. If we can get a clearer picture of her daily life, it could help us determine a pattern and catch the person who did this."

"So, you still don't know then?"

Anything other than the straight, hard truth wouldn't go over well with this woman. "No, ma'am, we don't. We have a few leads, but not enough viable evidence to pin this on a suspect."

"My baby was a good kid." Mrs. Washington's voice wavered for the first time. "She never got into trouble. She was a hard worker. Always did well in school. Why would anyone want to do this to her?"

"This might be a strange question, but was Sage's blood type O Negative?"

"Yeah." Mrs. Washington's eyebrows furrowed. "Why?"

"We think that could be one reason why she was chosen."

"Chosen." The other woman echoed Harris's words and a distant look came over her face. "But why?"

"We're still trying to figure that out." Harris leaned forward. "The night before she died, did you know where Sage was? Who she was with?"

Mrs. Washington's face hardened again. "My baby was a good kid."

"I'm not suggesting she wasn't." Harris worked to keep her voice gentle and even. "But if we know where she was or what she was up to, then it might help us narrow down our search area."

"She was downtown. She's older than my boys. A lot more responsible. She stayed home to save up money and help us around the house. She was never a big partier, but she liked to go downtown time to time, you know."

"With her friends?"

Mrs. Washington nodded her head. "Carla Rigsby and Sherri Coleman. She usually went out with them. Sometimes Lani Rodriguez."

"Do you have contact info for them?"

"I gave that to the first officer I spoke to."

"Any men in her life?"

Mrs. Washington laughed, but it sounded more like a sob. "No. She'd been trying online dating for a while. Never had much luck. She was too smart for any of them. Didn't want to settle."

"Smart girl." Harris offered a weak smile but it was not returned. "Do you know if she had a date on Friday or if she was just going out with her friends?"

"Like I said, she tried online dating, but it didn't work for her." She took a moment to calm down. "We didn't really talk about it. She was a private person. Never kept anything from me, I guess, but she was shy. Liked to wait until she was sure before she said anything. She always said it wasn't worth bringing anyone home if they weren't going to stick around for a while."

"Do you know what kind of guys she was into?"

"Sage was smart. Careful. She wouldn't have gone out with anyone who could've done this—who could've—" A sob escaped her mouth, and the woman looked away.

"Sometimes it's the people we least expect. This man could be charismatic. Unassuming. Completely ordinary. Boring, even. Sometimes we might act against our better judgment when we're attracted to someone."

Mrs. Washington looked back at Harris. The hardness had returned to her eyes. "I don't know who she was seeing. I don't know where she was. Talk to her friends."

"Ma'am—"

Mrs. Washington shouted toward the back of the house. "Jimmy! Get out here."

"Ma'am, please."

The other woman grabbed her cane and pushed herself to her feet. "I appreciate you coming out here, Detective Harris, but I have to continue making arrangements for my daughter's funeral." Jimmy entered the room and looked up at his mom expectantly. "Walk the detective to the door. Then we have to go."

Harris stood and produced her card. "If you think of anything else."

Mrs. Washington looked down at the card, back up at Harris, and then turned and ambled from the room. Young Jimmy pulled the card from Detective Harris's hand and tucked it in his pocket before leading her back through the kitchen.

At the door, Harris looked down at him. There was a sadness in his eyes that would take years to disappear if ever. "Do you know if your sister was seeing anyone?"

Jimmy looked over his shoulder before he answered. "No. But Carla would. She was always getting Sage in trouble."

"What kind of trouble?"

His eyes widened. "Nothing bad. Just coming home late.

Sometimes she was drunk. But she never drove when she was like that."

"She sounds like she was a good big sister."

"Yeah." His voice was far away. "She is. I mean, was."

Detective Harris didn't know what else to say, so she just thanked him and left, feeling like she was no closer to an answer than she was when she had arrived.

24

True to her word, Cassie did not call Harris over the next week. She half-expected the detective to call her to look at Sage's body, but several days passed with radio silence. Cassie had worn out her welcome.

The police department had bigger problems on their hands.

Ms. Campbell, the reporter who was always one step behind the police department, had confirmed with an "unidentified source" close to the investigation that the four women found over the last month had indeed all died in the same tragic manner—with their throats slashed and their hearts ripped out.

Of course, the public went wild. Every news station was talking about Savannah's latest serial killer. While the media played guessing games as to who could be behind these gruesome executions, the police department was busy dealing with nonsensical hotline tips and the press following Harris wherever she went.

David had called Cassie halfway through the week to give

her an update, but there wasn't much to say. They hadn't found anything new or different about the latest crime scene, and while it was confirmed that each woman's medical records had been changed to cover up that their blood type was O Negative, they were no closer to finding out who did it. The women had doctors at different hospitals so whoever was changing the records was able to hack into multiple systems across the city. David said they had their best people on the breach, but that it wasn't going to be easy to trace if the hacker knew how to cover his tracks.

Cassie told David about seeing Jessica Tran and getting a vision of her less than an hour before her death. He had taken note of what the medical van looked like but said vans like that were issued to several different hospitals in the area and that their own employees drive them. He searched through any missing vehicle reports, but there were none for medical transport vehicles.

Cassie had begged him to tell Harris to look at parking garages around the city to see if any of them housed medical vans, but she had refused to waste manpower on what she called a wild goose chase.

So, Cassie took matters into her own hands.

Every day that week, she picked a different parking garage and spent hours going through every level looking for something that matched up with what she saw in her vision. She knew it was a long shot. The driver could've changed where he parked the vehicle or changed what the van looked like by swapping out decals. But going on that wild goose chase felt a lot better than doing nothing.

And every day, she was disappointed. Parking in downtown Savannah wasn't cheap, even when she didn't stay long, and it hurt more when she continued to come up with nothing. There were plenty of white vans, none of which were medical transport vehicles. The ones that looked similar weren't enough of a match to warrant calling Harris or David.

When Friday night rolled around, Cassie didn't bother going home to change out of her work clothes and started her usual route around the city. With a Hardee's burger in one hand and a coffee in the other, she spent the next several hours trolling the streets of Savannah hoping and praying she could spot the van before the killer picked out his next victim.

What astounded her the most was that the nightlife in Savannah had not let up. The weather was warm without being oppressive, and Friday nights were always bound to be packed with tourists, students, and locals. She didn't expect the city to shut down because of a serial killer but was mildly surprised by how many people were out and about, enjoying a drink and a night on the town.

She stopped short of rolling down her windows and telling all the twenty-somethings to go home and lock their doors.

After her second dinner and third cup of coffee, she looked down at her dashboard. It was around midnight. The pit in her stomach grew tighter, and though she was doing her best, it didn't feel like enough.

Cassie pulled over along one of the side streets and parked her car. She tried to think backwards about this murder case. Harris theorized that the murders took place between midnight and two or three in the morning. It had to be late enough that most people wouldn't be at a park, and if they were, they wouldn't run into the middle of the woods if they saw something.

Cassie had a few more hours to figure out where to go.

She knew the killer used a medical transport van, which wouldn't stand out regardless of where it was parked. Doctors and nurses and medical couriers were automatically given a pass. As a society, we put our trust in them, and we rarely believed they could break that trust.

Then again, if Harris was right about her doctor theory, there'd be plenty of reason to think twice about trusting your doctor.

When Jessica Tran was taken to the medical transport van, it was parked in a garage several floors up. The killer did this to keep the vehicle off the street. Most parking garages had cameras at their entrances and exits, but if the killer switched jackets and wore a hat, no one would be able to tell if he entered in his personal vehicle and exited in the van.

Maybe Harris had already thought of that and had someone on her team look at the security footage, but Cassie couldn't be sure, and she wasn't about to call up the detective and tell her how to do her job. She would find some real evidence first.

And try not to gloat while she was at it.

Cassie drained her coffee and threw the empty cup on the floor of her car with the others. As she was about to lift her foot from the brake, she checked her rearview mirror and saw the back end of a white van drive by on the main road.

Her body reacted before her brain could comprehend what she had seen. She spun her vehicle around and gunned it toward the main road.

When she reached the intersection, she rolled through the stop sign and took a hard left. She weighed the consequences of getting pulled over by the police. On the one hand, she could tell them who she was and get them to pull over the van to check out the driver. On the other hand, it might cause enough of a distraction for the killer to get away. She leaned heavily in the direction of the killer getting away.

Cassie hit the gas and tried to distinguish the van from the other cars in front of her. In the middle of every intersection, she would slow down and peer in either direction to make sure the van hadn't made a turn. On every straightaway, she would speed up to pass as many cars as she could.

At the third intersection, she saw a white van get into the turn-only lane. Cassie weaved in between multiple cars and endured several middle fingers, but when she saw the words *Savannah Non-Emergency Medical Transport Van* on the side of the car, her heart caught in her chest and everything else disappeared.

Without a doubt, she knew she had found the killer. What would she do about it?

25

It took twenty seconds for reality to set in.

Cassie was sure she had found the killer on her own, but she didn't know what to do about it.

If it wasn't him and she was instead following some poor medical courier, that would make for an awkward encounter if she called the cops on the innocent man while the real killer had plenty of time to take his next victim.

But if it was him and she waited too long to act, she would never be able to forgive herself. However, she as dealing with a serial killer. If she managed to save his next victim, she very well could end up in the poor woman's place.

Against her better instincts, Cassie didn't reach for her phone. Instead, she trailed behind the transport van at a safe distance, hoping to God that her car looked inconspicuous enough to not draw his attention. All those action movies she had watched taught her a thing or two about how to tail a suspect. The time she had spent with actual police helped, too.

Cassie's palms started sweating when she realized they were driving further from Savannah. A sign for Lake Mayer caught her attention, and she slowed down enough to put more space between her and the van.

She knew where he was going.

Cassie looked down at her phone again. She could call Harris. Or David. She would have more luck with him. But something made her hesitate. What if she was wrong? What if she was wasting time? What if she pulled resources for a false alarm and another body showed up the next day?

Cassie followed at a distance until the van pulled off the parkway and onto East Montgomery Cross Road. She kept her distance and drove straight until he pulled into the park. She took the next right, pulled off the side of the road, and cut her engine. She would be slower on foot, but whoever was driving that van had to find a place to park, pull the girl out, and walk her to the woods to kill her.

Unless she was already dead.

Cassie pulled out her phone and texted David. She wrote out whatever came to mind.

Found the van. Followed it to Lake Mayer. Don't know if it's him. If you don't hear from me in 15, send the entire department.

Cassie knew it would give David an aneurysm, but she made sure her phone was on silent and tucked it into her back pocket. It was 12:24 a.m. She had until 12:40 to figure out what was going on and either call off the dogs or pray they got there in time to save her and his next victim.

On the upside, it took her about fifteen minutes to drive out there. It would take the cops less than ten once they were made aware of the situation.

Cassie jumped out of her car without a second thought and

ran toward the lake. Once she hit the path, she jogged until she reached the entrance, then stuck to the shadows as she walked along the parking lot. She reached the end of it and found the van.

At this point, her heart was pounding out of her chest. She didn't see any movement inside but hesitated to approach it. She slipped behind a tree and pulled out her phone, dimming the light enough to not give her away.

She had a barrage of missed calls and texts from David.

TELL ME YOU'RE JOKING.

CASSIE.

CASSIE YOU CAN'T BE SERIOUS.

I SWEAR TO GOD, QUINN, YOU BETTER ANSWER YOUR DAMN PHONE.

Cassie already had run a half mile. Ten of her fifteen minutes passed.

I'm fine, she texted back. *I'm following him. Staying at a distance. Will be safe. Text you in 10.*

No sooner had she hit send did David call her, but Cassie hit ignore and put her phone back in her pocket. She felt terrible for putting David in this situation, but she needed to do something. This was life and death. She was sure she was on the right track, but she needed evidence to prove this was the killer.

Cassie sprinted from tree to tree until she got close enough to the van to be sure no one was inside. When she peered through the windows, she didn't see anything of significance, and she didn't want to alert anyone by opening the door and risking the overhead light giving her away.

The whisper of a voice was carried on the wind. In the dead of night on the edge of a lake, everything carried, and while the traffic from the highway echoed across the open water, so did something else.

Cassie followed her instincts.

She took off at a dead sprint, staying on her toes and keeping to the paved path where the crunch of sticks and dead leaves and loose stones wouldn't give her away. She slowed down as she hit the first turn in the path and spotted two figures in the distance. She blinked and they disappeared into the trees.

They were too solid to be anything other than living, breathing people, and as brief a glimpse as it was, Cassie noticed one of the figures was half-carrying the other. Had he drugged her?

Cassie took off again, this time sticking to the grass on the outside of the path, closest to the road they came in on. If the killer spotted her, the cops might not have the chance to catch him again, and she refused to be the reason why he got away.

When Cassie reached the edge of the trees, she pulled her phone out. She had run about a mile, and her extra ten minutes were up. She had more texts and missed calls from David, but she didn't bother reading any of them.

Two figures entering the woods, Cassie typed out. *Send help.*

Doubt entered her mind as soon as she hit send, but logic battled with anxiety and won out. At this point, the chances were low that this wasn't the killer with the medical van dragging a woman into the woods in the dead of night. Everything was right in front of her.

She had to figure out how to stall him until the cops arrived.

Cassie tucked her phone back in her pocket before David could respond. She took a deep breath and ventured into the trees, grateful that she had worn her flats to work today instead of heels.

The canopy offered by the trees darkened the woods much more than the open air, but her eyes adjusted in a few seconds. Pulling her phone out to use the flashlight would have been an idiotic move, so she moved through the forest as quickly and quietly as she could, despite the brambles digging into her legs.

The voices carried by the wind earlier were louder and Cassie could hear movement ahead. She slowed down and readjusted her trajectory, though it was hard to get a precise direction amidst the trees.

A few minutes later, a light switched on to her right and Cassie froze. It was far enough away that she didn't worry about being noticed, but when it swept toward her, she ducked behind a tree, just in case. The noise she made could be construed as that of an animal, but she doubted she would be mistaken for a deer if the light landed on her.

Once the beam turned in the other direction, Cassie took the opportunity to sprint from tree to tree, keeping a wide berth but circling in closer. Her heart was pounding against her ribcage like a sledgehammer against sand and she was terrified that he would be able to hear it.

When the flashlight stopped moving, so did Cassie. She took a few deep breaths and knelt, searching with her hands until she found a branch thick enough to do some real damage.

When a voice spoke again, Cassie realized she was much closer than she anticipated. This time it was the girl and she sounded confused and exhausted.

"Where are we?" She sounded like she had been crying.

"I told you," the man said, his voice calm, "we're going to have a campfire."

"I don't want to have a campfire," the girl said.

"You don't want to make some s'mores?"

"No." The girl was crying. "I want to go home. Please. I'm tired."

"Don't worry," the man said. "It'll be over soon."

26

"Where are we?" the girl asked again.

"You wanted a campfire, remember?"

The man's voice was gentle and coaxing, but Cassie was starting to pick up on some anxiety, too. It was masked well, but something was off. Was he worried about being caught? Could serial killers feel remorse?

"I don't feel good."

"Well, lucky for you, I'm a doctor," the man replied. "Come on, I'll give you a checkup. Won't that be fun?"

Instead of answering, the woman threw up. Cassie took advantage of the distraction to move closer, praying that the crunch of leaves underfoot wouldn't give her away. She was still several feet away, but she could at least see the two people in front of her. She caught a glimpse of them and ducked behind a tree. The man was tall and trim with broad shoulders and muscled arms. He was the man from her vision. The woman was short with bright pink hair. She was dressed like she had been out partying. She looked strange against the backdrop of the forest.

"It's so dark out here," she said.

"I'll light the fire soon. Why don't you sit down?"

"I don't want to get dirty," the girl complained, but Cassie heard rustling leaves and assumed the girl sat down anyway.

Cassie gripped the branch harder. Her hands were starting to ache. Her legs were bleeding. Her pants had ripped half a dozen times. She was aware of these sensations, but they registered in the deepest part of her mind.

Nothing mattered except what was right in front of her.

Cassie decided to take another chance and peer around the tree again. One quick glance was enough to get a picture of what was going on a few feet in front of her. The woman was kneeling on the ground, clutching her purse to her chest. Cassie could see that she was wearing shorts and a tank top. Her arm was bleeding from rubbing up against a low-hanging branch, but she didn't appear to notice.

The man was standing behind the woman. He was holding the flashlight under his arm and he had a bucket in one hand and a toolbox in the other. Cassie shivered, knowing for a fact that the bucket was for the woman's blood and the toolbox contained the bone saw that would soon open her chest if Cassie didn't do something first. What other torture devices might be found in there?

Cassie leaned to the side, trying to get a better view of what was in front of her, but as she did, a branch snapped underfoot. She had a split second to duck back behind the tree when the man whirled around and put the spotlight on her hiding spot.

Every muscle in her body tensed as she waited and waited

for the beam to move away. She didn't dare breathe lest she give away her position. But instead of thinking it was nothing but a squirrel, the man started walking forward, closer to Cassie.

As the light beam bounced with every step he took, Cassie's brain was a whirlwind of thought. Should she jump out and surprise him? Should she wait until he was next to the tree and attack? What side would he walk up to? Would he stop and turn around? If he did that, she would have a better chance of getting the upper hand.

But what would she do after she attacked him? If she landed the perfect blow, she would only have a few seconds to get to the girl and drag her away. But since the woman was drugged, she wouldn't be able to keep up with Cassie. Or she would be afraid of Cassie and try to get away. Maybe even try to go back to the man.

And if Cassie didn't land the perfect blow, she would have to struggle with the killer, a losing proposition. He was bigger and stronger than she was. She had taken self-defense classes after being attacked by Novak, but she was no expert. And those classes were always about how to get the upper hand and run away, not how to take out a serial killer and free his victim.

The beam from the flashlight stopped bouncing. Cassie heard the man turn around and allowed herself to breathe again. It was now or never.

Cassie lunged forward from her hiding spot and swung the branch back at the same time. The man in front of her twisted around at the noise and Cassie didn't hesitate to bring her arm down toward his face. When the branch connected with the man's skull, it vibrated in Cassie's hands, sending a violent ripple throughout her arm from wrist to shoulder, and sending the man sprawling.

But it didn't knock him out.

The man scrambled to his feet and put himself between Cassie and the woman on the ground.

"Who are you?" Spit flew from his mouth.

Cassie saw his face in good lighting for the first time. She wasn't sure what she was expecting, but it certainly wasn't the man who stood in front of her. He was in his late thirties or early forties and had thick brown hair that was coiffed to perfection on top of his head. He was handsome with brown eyes and a strong jawline. He was dressed in a button-down shirt and slacks and his shoes were neat and polished.

He looked normal. If she had met him at a bar, she would've been flattered if he had flirted with her. But his confusion soon gave way to an animalistic fury that lay under the surface of his well-kept normalcy.

She wondered how someone capable of that much hate and anger could ever go to work with the intent to bring comfort and solace to his patients and their loved ones.

"Who are you?" he repeated, rage building.

The current situation wasn't looking great for Cassie. She was convinced she wouldn't be able to go toe-to-toe with him in a fight. Her best chance of survival was either getting the upper hand with her makeshift weapon or stalling him long enough for the police to get there.

"My name's Cassie." She spoke in as calm a voice as she could muster. She took a step to her right, hoping she could turn him around and get closer to the woman. "What's your name?"

"Stop moving." He pointed the bright light into Cassie's eyes, and she had to look at his feet to keep her sense of where he was. "What are you doing here?"

"I followed you," she said. "Didn't you notice me?"

He took a step toward her. "Does anyone know you're here?"

"No," Cassie lied. "No, they don't. Please, let us go and I promise I won't say anything."

"No, no, you've seen too much."

"I haven't seen anything," Cassie said. She took an imperceptible step to her right. "Please, I want to get my friend and leave."

"She said she was out by herself tonight."

"She was." Cassie hoped her lie would hold for another minute or two. "She didn't know I came out tonight. I spotted her, but I didn't want to interrupt you two. But I saw her leave with you, and I got worried."

The man's face turned a darker shade of red. "You're lying."

Cassie didn't have any warning when he lunged at her. She threw herself to the side and swung at him again. This time, the branch hit his shoulder and snapped in half. What was left behind was short but sharp on one end. The man stumbled but lunged again and tackled her to the ground. She landed with a grunt. Despite the air being knocked out of her, she managed to stab him with the sharp end of the stick. He hollered in pain and backhanded her across the face hard enough to make her world go dark for a split second.

"You bitch."

Cassie couldn't move. The man positioned himself on top of her and pinned her arms with his legs. The pain was excruciating, and no matter how much she bucked and kicked, she couldn't knock him off.

When he threw the branch to the side, Cassie was grateful he hadn't decided to end her life then and there. But the relief was short-lived. He wrapped his large hands around her neck and squeezed until she couldn't breathe. His grip was so tight, she couldn't scream for help.

The last thing she saw before she passed out was his wicked grin and the pure malice in his eyes.

27

The pressure released from Cassie's neck, and she coughed and gagged as air was restored to her lungs. Cassie looked up in time to see the young woman swinging the doctor's toolbox at his head. It connected with a sickening thud, and the man toppled off her with a grunt. His limp body collapsed on the ground and folded onto itself.

Her neck was throbbing—it would bruise—and her throat was sore. She swallowed past a lump and winced again, fearing the mark that would be left. How would she explain this one at the museum?

The woman stumbled past Cassie and dropped the toolbox. It burst open and sent tools flying. Cassie lurched forward and grabbed a knife at the same time the man regained consciousness and his own balance and scooped up a small device with a round blade on one end.

A bone saw.

The flashlight was on the ground now, half covered by

detritus from the forest floor, but still illuminating all three of them in a warm cone like stage lighting, enough that it was easy to keep track of the killer. Cassie put herself between him and the woman who sank back down to her knees and was crying again.

"Please," Cassie said. The word scraped along her throat, she had to swallow to ease the pain. "Don't do this."

"I don't like complications."

"I don't have to be a complication," Cassie said. The pain in her throat was subsiding, but it still felt raw and tender. "Let us go."

Cassie wasn't sure what she would do if he took off into the woods. He might escape, but she and the victim would both be safe. And Cassie had seen enough of him that she would be able to identify him from a photograph. Unless he could disappear from the face of the earth, his life was over.

"I can't let you go." The glow of the flashlight made his smile look more menacing. "But I promise I'll make it quick."

"Will you drain my blood too?" Cassie had to keep him talking. "It's not O Negative, if that's what you're wondering."

"How do you know about that?"

"The police know." Cassie was playing with fire. "What I'm interested in is, why? What do you need the blood for?"

The man scoffed. "It's not for me."

"Then for who? Who are you sacrificing these women for? Why?"

He looked at her like she was an ant beneath his boot. "That's not a question I'm going to answer."

Cassie decided to change tactics. "How could you do this? You're a doctor. You're supposed to keep people alive."

He laughed, and for the first time, it seemed like there was actual emotion on his face. "Do you know one of the first lessons I learned as a doctor? Humans are fragile. We think we're the apex predator, but all we can rely on is our brain, and most of our species can't even do that."

"So, you choose to kill people instead?"

"I didn't choose this." He took a step forward. His voice quieted. "I didn't choose this. I'm doing what I have to. That's what we're taught as doctors. Save who you can. *Choose.* Play God. If you lose someone, move on. There are more to save."

"But you're not choosing to save one person over another. You're choosing to kill one person over another. Doesn't the Hippocratic Oath mean anything to you?"

"Am I?" He smiled again and it looked wrong. He didn't look deranged. He was in complete control. Measured. It shook Cassie to her core. "Who knows you're here?"

"No one."

"See, you've already lied to me once, so I'm not inclined to believe you. Let's find out, shall we?"

Keeping eye contact, he knelt and picked up something off the ground. It was her phone. It must've fallen out of her pocket when they'd struggled. A pit formed in her stomach. Even if she could get away, she wouldn't be able to call someone. She would be on her own in the middle of the woods.

She hoped David received her last text and had already sent the police.

"Ah, David. Is he your boyfriend? He seems very concerned." He made eye contact with Cassie. "You shouldn't have told him where we were. You know that, right? I'm not a sadist, but my anger does get the best of me sometimes."

"Please—"

"Shut up. I need to think."

"Look, you can't take us both." Cassie infused her voice with as much calm as she could muster, though her hand holding the knife was trembling. "One of us is going to get away and then you're screwed."

"She's still out of it," the man said. "And will be for a while. If she runs, she's not going to get far."

"Do you think you can do that before the cops get here?" Cassie asked. "You need her blood, right? And her heart? You think you can kill me, kill her, and still make it out of here?"

"There's one way to find out."

The man switched on the bone saw and lunged for Cassie. She had a split second to dive out of the way and her first thought was to keep a grip on the blade in her hand. She landed on the ground and felt sharp pain ripple outward from her knee. She had landed on a rock. She rolled to the side, hopping back up on her feet despite the sharp pain in her leg.

It took her a moment to orient herself, but by the time she found the doctor again, he had pulled the woman to her feet and held the saw to her neck.

Cassie made the wrong move.

"Please," Cassie begged. "Don't do this."

"Did you call the police?"

Cassie didn't know if it was better to lie or tell the truth. She let the silence stretch on.

"Answer me!" the doctor yelled, moving the saw closer to the woman's throat.

"Yes! Yes!" Cassie locked eyes with the woman. They both had tears running down their cheeks. "They're on their way. You're not going to get away with this. You already have four bodies on your hands, you don't need more."

"You're right," he said. "I already have four on my hands.

What's two more? I'll already be getting consecutive life sentences if I don't get the electric chair."

"You said it yourself, you're not a sadist." Cassie's mind was working at warp speed. "What do you want?"

The flashlight's dull beam illuminated the confusion on his face. "What?"

"I know half the police department. What do you want?"

Cassie had spent a long time being afraid—of Novak, of men, of the dark, of life. A lot of therapy and a great deal of time had helped her work through most of her issues, but she'd be lying if she didn't admit she woke up in a cold sweat every once in a while, terrified that she was back in that graveyard or back in the basement of that house when Novak had tried to kill her a second time.

But now? She felt the calm wash over her. She didn't have a choice. She was fighting for her life and the life of this woman she had never met. There was no room for error.

"Who are you?" the doctor asked again. The difference this time was that he seemed interested.

Cassie caught movement out of the corner of her eye, but she refused to look away from the man in front of her. "My name is Cassie Quinn. I'm—I'm a psychic."

The doctor laughed. "You've got to be kidding me."

"I'm not." Cassie licked her lips. "I've seen every single one of your victims. First, Elizabeth. Then Hannah. I saw Sage's dead body the morning after she was killed. Then I saw Jessica's ghost. She's the one who told me how to find you. She showed me the van in a parking garage."

The look on the doctor's face was a strange mixture of fear and incredulity. "Impossible."

"How else do you explain how I found you? How else would

I know you were driving that van?" Cassie kept talking. She kept saying whatever came to mind. Anything to stretch the seconds into minutes. Engaging his curiosity had the effect of keeping his intelligent mind working, guessing, trying to figure out who this woman in front of him really was. "You've been meticulous this entire time. You left no evidence behind. Look at me. I'm not a cop. If I were, I'd have come here with a gun. I'm just some woman."

The man opened his mouth to say something, but the words didn't come out. Harris's voice rang out through the darkness. "Savannah PD. Put down your weapon."

Several flashlights switched on, illuminating Cassie, the doctor, and his victim in a swath of bright light.

28

Cassie dropped the knife. Tension drained from her body. Blood drained from her head and she felt as though she were about to collapse to the ground. The hum of the bone saw faded until all she heard were the crickets and labored breaths surrounding them.

Then the woods erupted in chaos.

Several officers, including Harris, moved in on the doctor and his victim, separating the two. They pushed the doctor to his knees and handcuffed him while a pair of EMTs emerged from the trees to check out the woman, who was shaking and crying in earnest.

David appeared by Cassie's side like he had materialized out of thin air.

"Are you hurt?"

Cassie shook her head no. It was all she could manage. Her voice had left her. Her knees shook uncontrollably. She sunk to the ground and David stayed with her the entire way down.

"Jesus Christ," he whispered. "You scared me."

Another EMT ran over to Cassie and looked her over. She heard the paramedic talking with David, but the words sounded far away. She felt a cool sensation on her legs and looked down to see a woman covering the worst of her cuts with gel and several small bandages.

"Is she okay?" Cassie heard her own voice as if it belonged to someone else. "The woman, is she okay?"

"She's fine," David said. "You saved her life."

The EMT threw a blanket over Cassie's shoulders and shined a light in her eyes. She inspected the bruise forming around Cassie's neck. When she looked back up at David, the EMT said, "No major damage. She'll be fine."

"Thank God." David's hunched shoulders retreated.

Harris appeared out of the darkness and knelt in front of Cassie. Her face was a strange combination of concern and anger and confusion. It took her a few minutes to find any words.

"Are you okay?"

"I'm fine," Cassie said. As the adrenaline faded, she regained sensation in her arms and legs, and she was grateful the paramedic had taken care of the deeper cuts. The tender areas around her neck would take longer to heal.

"You shouldn't have come here by yourself." Harris's words were controlled. She was speaking just above a whisper, but her voice still held all its power. "That was incredibly stupid."

"I know."

"Cassie, I—" Harris broke off and took a few seconds to gather herself. "Cassie, I'm thrilled you're okay, but what you did tonight... You should've called me."

"I know. It didn't go as planned."

"And how were you planning it to go?"

"I-I don't know." Cassie put her head in her hands. The reality of the situation dawned on her. "I didn't think. I reacted. I didn't want to bother you if it was nothing, but I knew I couldn't let it go."

"How did you find the van?"

"Coincidence."

Harris surprised Cassie by laughing. "I'm trying to figure out if you're the luckiest person alive or the *unluckiest.*"

"If you figure that out," David said, "let me know."

"Why would you come here by yourself, Cassie?" Harris asked.

"I wanted to see if he could be a suspect." Cassie pulled the blanket around her shoulders. "When I got here, I saw him leading her into the woods. I couldn't let him go and risk not stopping him. I figured I could stall him long enough for you guys to get here."

"You messaged David but not me."

"You were pretty angry the last time we spoke."

Harris blew out a big breath and placed a hand on Cassie's shoulder. "I was. I'm sorry about that. This case has been stressful."

"I never intended to add to your stress."

"I know." Harris laughed again, this time with a touch of hysteria. "I still don't understand you. I'm not sure I believe what you do is real, but I'd be an idiot to not see that it gets results."

"You're not the first person to say that to me."

"That doesn't surprise me." Harris looked up at David. "What about you? Did you believe her the first time around?"

Cassie answered for him. "Oh, definitely not. He threw me in jail. Overnight."

Harris smiled. "Really?"

"I did," David said.

"Yeah. I don't blame him. It was a rough case. I was going crazy seeing all the victims. I didn't know what to do. I wanted someone to listen to me."

"And he did?" Harris said.

"Eventually." Cassie shrugged. "Took him a while, but yeah. We worked on another case after that. And then another. He saw I wasn't nuts. Started to trust me."

Harris stood and the other two copied her movements. "Tell me, Detective Klein. How long did it take for you to start believing in ghosts?"

"Not sure I do." David looked over at Cassie, and a gentle smile made its way to his face. "But I believe in her."

Cassie allowed the warmth of his words to fill her up. She reached out and squeezed his arm. "Thank you for coming for me."

"You're welcome." The smile faded. "But if you ever pull something like that again, I'm throwing you back in a jail cell, Quinn."

"I get the feeling you're quite the handful." Harris looked at Cassie.

All Cassie could do was shrug. "I bend the rules when I don't think there's another option."

Harris's eyes sparkled. "I'm pretty sure that's what vigilantes say, and they're frowned upon."

"I just want to help," Cassie said.

Over the last few days, she had struggled with her abilities and how her future would be impacted if they didn't go away.

As comforting as the idea was to never see another dead person, she knew she would miss it sooner or later. It was on days like this that it all felt worth it.

Cassie peered around Harris and saw the EMTs loading the young woman on a stretcher. She looked alert and she was talking with the paramedics and one of the other officers.

"Her name is Katie," Harris said. "You saved her life."

Cassie let the bubble of emotion overwhelm her for a moment and tears fell from the corners of her eyes. She would've made a million different choices if she had to do it all over again, but she couldn't deny that it felt good hearing those words.

"You did a stupid thing tonight, Quinn," David's voice softened. "But it was a good thing, too."

"I don't disagree, but let's not make it a habit, okay?" Harris said.

"I'll try not to," Cassie replied.

Harris stood. "We should get back to the precinct." She turned to Cassie. "We'll need to take your statement and I want to get started on questioning this asshole sooner rather than later."

29

David pulled up to the precinct and put the sedan in park. Cassie opened her eyes when she felt the vehicle stop. She allowed the cool night air from the open window to calm her down from the night's events.

"Cassie." David turned to her, speaking for the first time since they had gotten into the car. "You scared me tonight."

"I'm sorry. I didn't mean to."

"I'm happy you reached out to me," David hesitated.

"But?"

"I've known you for a long time. You're smart, and I don't believe for a second that you're incapable of taking care of yourself. But you can't take on the world alone."

"I'm not—"

David held up his hand. "Maybe I'm crossing a line here, and maybe I'm reading the room wrong, but if I don't say it, I'm going to regret it."

"I'm listening."

"You mean a lot to me and Lisa. I've seen the real you over these past few years, and I know without a doubt that you're one of the best people I've ever met. You're selfless and brave and good, right down to your soul. But you also scare the shit out of me sometimes."

"I do?"

David nodded his head and Cassie caught a glimpse of a tear in his eye. "You have a gift that can help so many people, but sometimes I think you forget to help yourself. It's okay to want to take a break once in a while. It's okay if you fail. I learned a long time ago that I can't save everyone. That sometimes keeps me up at night, but it also keeps me sane. Something tells me you struggle with the same thing."

Cassie didn't know what to say. She nodded.

"You have a profound effect on people," he continued. "Harris has known you for a couple of days and you've already changed her."

"I have?"

"She'll never admit it but yeah. You have." He wiped a tear away. "I guess what I'm saying is that sometimes you're like a candle that's burning too bright. You add a lot of light to this world, but I'm terrified you're going to burn out too soon. I know you're always going to get mixed up in cases like this, but you can't go running in there half-cocked. You have to be smart about it. You have to let people help you."

Cassie placed a hand on David's arm. "I'm sorry. I wasn't thinking about anything other than trying to stop this guy."

He patted her hand. "I want you to keep helping people for as long as you're up to the task. But you must take care of yourself occasionally, too."

"I'm trying." Cassie blew out a large breath. This was not the conversation she was expecting to have tonight. "After Novak, when all the ghosts left, I didn't feel as relieved as I thought I would. I felt empty. I was on edge. Like at any minute they would come back unannounced."

"And they did."

"But it felt good to help tonight." She stared out the windshield and watched as police officers came and went from the building. "It feels good to know that I can help bring peace to Elizabeth, Hannah, and the others. It feels good to know I saved Katie's life tonight. I love my job at the museum, and I wouldn't give it up for the world, but my abilities make me who I am."

"It sounds like you're trying to convince yourself more than you're trying to convince me."

Cassie's laugh was watery. Tears gathered at the corners of her eyes. "That's true. It's not always easy, but tonight reminded me how strong I can be. It was a good feeling."

"I'm glad. Don't do it again."

Cassie laughed, and she was relieved when David joined in with her. "I'll try to be better. I promise. No more late-night texts about hunting down a serial killer on my own."

"I don't think that's too much to ask," David said. "C'mon. Let's get you situated. I need to call Lisa so she can stop worrying about you."

"Tell her I'm sorry, too."

David led Cassie into the precinct where she was passed off to another officer. It was the cop she had seen at Sage's crime scene, the one who had talked to the reporter. Now that she was up close, she could see how young he was. He couldn't have been on the force for more than a year, two at the most.

Cassie was taken to an interrogation room so she could get her statement down as soon as possible. The walls of the room pressed in on her and she remembered the countless times she had been somewhere similar. The bad memories stuck out.

It didn't take long for her to write out and sign her statement. She and the rookie went over it twice to ensure she had included every detail. And she had.

She started at the graveyard and the vision from Jessica and went on to her decision to search downtown Savannah for the medical transport van. While it would make things more complicated in court, given the way they stumbled upon the evidence, they caught the killer red-handed and that was the most important fact.

When the rookie was satisfied, he left the room and was replaced by David.

"How're you holding up?" he asked.

"Pretty good, all things considered. I'd like to get out of this room, though."

David stepped to the side and held the door open for her. "How do you feel about watching the interrogation?"

Cassie paused in the hallway outside the door. "Really? Harris is okay with that?"

"She suggested it," David said. "Said it was the least she could do. Might help you with some resolution."

"Speaking of, how's Katie?"

"Katie is fine. She'll make a full recovery. She's an incredibly lucky woman and I think she's aware of how close she came to death tonight. That's not something she'll get over soon, as you're well aware of, but she's alive. That's the important part. She's grateful to you, by the way."

Cassie smiled. It felt good to hear that. "Is Lisa mad at me?"

David chuckled. "She's relieved you're fine and that I made it back in one piece. She's glad we caught the bastard, but I'm sure she'll have some strong words for you when you see her next."

"Sunday roast?" Cassie asked. They hadn't had one of those in a while, but it seemed like a good time to pick back up on the tradition.

"Sounds good to me."

David opened another door, and he and Cassie filed into a dimly lit room. There were two other officers inside, including the Chief of Police. Cassie had run into her a few times, but they were not friends. By the tight-lipped smile she gave Cassie, Cassie was certain she was aware of the night's events.

Cassie's attention was taken over by what was happening on the other side of the two-way mirror. The doctor was seated on one side of a shiny metal table with his hands cuffed in front of him. A man in a crisp navy suit sat next to him.

David leaned down to whisper in Cassie's ear. "He lawyered up the second he was arrested."

"He'd be dumb not to with all the evidence against him," Cassie said.

At that moment, the door to the interrogation room opened and Harris walked in. She was followed by another detective. He was tall and lean, but his imposing figure was offset by his boyish features. He had sandy hair and a clean-shaven face. Something about him screamed *army* to Cassie, but she had not met him before.

"I'm Detective Adelaide Harris and this is my colleague Detective Payton Beauregard." Harris's demeanor was vastly different from how Cassie had ever seen it. She had a confident, almost arrogant air about her, and she seemed so at ease with the situation at hand.

"I love this part," David said wistfully.

Harris arranged a stack of folders in front of her and sat down, folding her hands across the top of them. The other detective mirrored her movements, though his stiffness implied he had little experience sitting across from a serial killer.

Harris didn't bother wasting time. She turned to the lawyer with a genuine smile on her face. "Mr. White, it's always good to see you, though I'm a bit surprised you're here. I know you're used to touting the so-called innocence of your clients, but it's going to be pretty difficult to do that in this case."

Mr. White's smile was as genuine. "I'm going to cut straight to the chase, Detective Harris. My client is willing to provide you with a full confession in exchange for a reduced sentence."

Harris laughed, shocked by the audacity of the statement. "It's not going to be difficult to prove he committed all four murders, Mr. White. Why would we consider your offer?"

Mr. White leaned back in his chair. "My client was coerced. To have his charge reduced, he's willing to provide you with every detail of this particular, ah, *situation,* as well as information on the man who's been *blackmailing* him."

Harris looked between Mr. White and the doctor. She opened her mouth, but no words came out.

Mr. White leaned forward again. "Shall we get started?"

30

"Whenever you're ready, Dr. Langford," Harris said.

Cassie took a step closer to the interrogation window and looked at the doctor for the first time since their standoff in the woods. He was, in fact, a handsome man, but there was something about his eyes. Something missing. They looked like shark eyes. Cold. Dark. Void of empathy.

Not for the first time that night, Cassie wondered how someone like that could be a doctor.

Langford turned to his lawyer. "I don't know about this. It doesn't feel right."

Harris leaned forward. "Dr. Langford, it is far from a little-known fact that I'm not the biggest fan of Mr. White, but I can assure you that he's an extremely capable lawyer. He always has his best interests in mind and therefore his clients' as well. If he has advised you to provide us with an explanation as to why you murdered four women and attempted to kill two more, take the advice. If you don't, I can guarantee we'll be able to pull enough evidence from your van in order to nail you to the wall. Several walls, in fact."

Langford glared at Harris for a second or two while mulling over his options. His steepled hands separated and fingertips fell to the table. He provided her a tight smile. "Very well. Where should I start?"

"Tell them about Lucy," Mr. White said. "Start at the beginning."

"I had been dating Lucy Sitwell for about two years. She found out I had been cheating on her with one of the nurses at work, and when she came to confront me, we had a big fight. She tried to leave, I grabbed her arm, she yanked it away, and proceeded to fall down the stairs at my house. I heard her neck crack when she hit the bottom. Her head started bleeding. Just from the sound, I already knew she couldn't be saved."

Cassie put a hand over her mouth. "My God," she whispered. "He said it like he's reading from a textbook. He doesn't even care."

Harris nodded at Beauregard, who started taking notes, and turned back to Langford. "How long ago was this?"

"About six weeks."

"Did you report her death to the police?"

"No."

"Why not?"

"It would've ruined my reputation." Langford's voice was easy, relaxed. "If I reported her death to the police, I would've looked like a suspect. It would've been easy enough to discover I had been cheating, easy enough to see she had shown up to confront me. Even if I was not arrested or convicted, my colleagues would've always wondered if I'd done it. That would've impacted my work at the hospital."

"What did you do instead?"

For the first time, Langford looked uncomfortable. "I chose to cover it up."

"How?"

"I buried her body in the woods on the edge of my property in the middle of the night. I cleaned up my house, made sure it was spotless. I took all of her clothes and everything she'd left behind and put them in her car, and I drove her car back to her apartment."

"That same night?"

"Yes."

"What did you do next?" Harris asked. She glanced over at Beauregard's notes and apparently satisfied, returned her unflinching gaze to Langford.

"I made sure no one was around, and then I packed a bag and made it look like she'd decided to leave town. Her sister lives in Oregon. They were always emailing back and forth. I sent her a message as Lucy saying she needed to get away and that she was going to drive up to visit her. Lucy was always talking about wanting to take a cross country trip."

"I take it you had no interest in that?"

"It seems like a waste of time," Langford said coolly. "If I wanted to visit the west coast, it would be California and I'd fly there. I'd also make sure to go alone."

"Did you care about Lucy?" Harris asked. "At all?"

Langford smiled, but it didn't reach his eyes. "Of course, I cared about her. We were a good fit. She was good looking. Easy to please."

"You mean easy to manipulate?"

"Detective Harris," Mr. White leaned forward, "please don't

put words into my client's mouth. He's cooperating with your investigation."

"We'll see about that," Harris said. "What did you do after you sent the email?"

"I drove her car an hour west. Left it in a gas station parking lot. Then I called one of my buddies and asked him to pick me up."

"Your friend didn't think that was strange?"

Langford looked at Harris like she was a simpleton. "We were always doing stuff like that. Going out, getting drunk. Picking up women and going back to their place. We have a strict *no questions asked* policy."

"And your friend will be able to corroborate your story?"

"Colt Morrison. He'll tell you the same thing I did."

"We'll be sure to find out," Harris said. "What about Lucy's friends and family? They must've been worried about her."

"Her sister tried calling her the next day."

"Then what happened?"

"Obviously, she didn't pick up."

"Mr. Langford, do I need to remind you that you are in an incredible amount of trouble? Your life, as you know it, is over. I am your best shot at getting what you want from this. I suggest you use less sarcasm."

Langford rolled his eyes. "Of course, Detective. My apologies."

Harris brushed it off. "Did Lucy's sister call the police?"

"Yes." Langford's tone was one of forced civility. "They paid me a visit. I was upfront about the fight, but I said she left. I played the part of a grieving boyfriend, regretful of having cheated on her."

"Were you aware of whether they suspected foul play?"

"They probably did, but you'd have to talk to the cops who interviewed me. Given my profession, I was afforded the benefit of the doubt. As far as I know, the investigation is ongoing."

"And Lucy's family?"

"Her sister tracked me down at work, asked all sorts of questions."

"Did she suspect you?"

"I don't think so. Like I said, being a doctor has its perks."

"Did your colleagues have anything to say? Your friends? Did Colt Morrison suspect you?"

"Colt's an idiot. We were pre-med together, but he couldn't cut it. Dropped out and became a real estate agent. Like I said, he doesn't ask questions."

"And your colleagues?"

"They felt bad for me." Langford looked proud of himself. "I was grieving. Got some time off out of it, too."

"And the nurse you were sleeping with?"

"She didn't care. She knew I had a girlfriend at the time. She thought I had bad luck. Made her feel bad for me. Worked out in my favor."

Harris looked disgusted.

Cassie leaned over to David. "This guy is a joke. He watched his girlfriend die and has no remorse."

"I wouldn't be surprised if he pushed her," David said. "But it's going to be hell trying to prove that given his story."

"Why is he admitting to all of this anyway? He knows he's going to prison."

"He would've gone to prison regardless. Better to go for covering up your girlfriend's death—accidental or not—than to take the blame for killing those four women."

"But he did kill those four women," Cassie said.

Harris spoke again, cutting off whatever David was about to say.

"I assume you'll be telling us the exact location for Lucy's body?"

Mr. White answered for his client. "My client is more than willing to cooperate in any way deemed necessary."

"So, you've said. Many times."

Harris turned back to Langford. "So, I want to get this right. Your girlfriend catches you cheating and confronts you at your house. You get into a fight and accidentally push her down the—"

"I didn't push her." Langford's face was red. "I'm not a common criminal, Detective Harris. Please don't treat me like one."

"My mistake," Harris looked pleased with herself. "You get into a fight and she *falls* down the stairs. Then, instead of calling the cops and reporting the accident, you decide to bury her body and make it look like she left town."

"An action my client regrets," Mr. White said.

"Of course." Harris wasn't convinced. "And when the police showed up with questions, you doubled down on your story. Is this all correct?"

"More or less, yes," Langford said.

"So, I guess the question is, how does any of this tie to the reason you decided to kill four other women?"

"I didn't decide anything." Langford sat up straight in his chair. "Like I said, I was coerced."

"And who coerced you?"

"Oh, I have no idea." Langford was dead serious. "He hasn't told me who he is."

31

Harris kept her composure, but Cassie could tell she was fighting to keep her frustration at bay. She plastered a smile on her face and turned to the lawyer. "Mr. White, if your client is wasting my time, so help me—"

"I assure you, Detective Harris, he is quite serious. As he relayed the story to me, a letter showed up a week later. The sender knew my client had buried his girlfriend in his backyard and proceeded to mislead the police every step of the way in their investigation into her disappearance."

"How did he know?" Harris asked.

"Not a clue." Langford's voice was cold. "He didn't stop and explain his evil plan before he told me to commit murder for him."

Harris leaned back in her seat and crossed one leg over the other. "All right, start from the beginning."

Langford looked over at his lawyer again. When White nodded, Langford turned back to the detectives.

"A week after Lucy died, a letter showed up in the mail. No return address. It pretty much said he knew what had happened. He told me that if I wanted it to stay a secret, I had to do a few things for him."

"That was it?" Harris asked.

"That was it. A few days later, another letter showed up. This one told me to go to the junkyard and pay cash for an old medical transport van that was about to get scrapped."

"Given your mode of transportation, I assume you did it."

"At the time, it seemed like a small price to pay to keep my secret, uh, buried, for lack of a better word."

Harris's smile was tight. "Did another letter come after that?"

"Next, he told me to steal some tools from the hospital, including an electric bone saw. Again, it didn't seem like a big deal."

"When did it start becoming a big deal?"

"A few days later, he sent me a picture in the mail, along with a name and some basic information."

"One of your victims?" Harris asked.

"One of the blackmailer's victims," Mr. White clarified. "My client was—"

"Coerced, yeah I got it." Harris looked back at Langford. "Who was it?"

"Hannah Williams. This guy told me he'd set her up on a date through one of the dating apps using a fake profile. When that guy stood her up, I would swoop in and flirt with her. Then I'd drug her drink, get her to leave with me, and transport her using the van. We'd go to whatever park I could get into without being noticed and slit her throat, collect the blood, and cut out her heart."

"Just like that?" Harris asked. "Why not admit to Lucy's accidental death and go to the cops with the information you had on the blackmailer?"

"I had no information," Langford said. "And I was scared for my life."

"Scared for your life?" Harris looked as incredulous as Cassie felt. "Did the blackmailer threaten your life? Other than when he told you he'd turn you in for Lucy's death?"

"He made it clear that he would ruin me if I didn't do what he said."

David growled. "Bullshit." He was shaking his head. "This guy gets off on it."

"Gets off on what?" Cassie whispered.

"Look at how calm he's been this whole time. He's like a freaking robot. He deals in life and death every day at the hospital. Probably doesn't bat an eye at it anymore. I bet he killed his girlfriend and liked the rush of getting away with it. Even if the letters are real, I doubt he put up much of a fight when this guy came to him."

"Klein, that's enough," the Police Chief said. Cassie had almost forgotten she was there. "Save it for when we're building the case against him."

David shook his head as he chewed his lower lip.

"What did you do after you killed Hannah Williams?" Harris asked.

"I put the blood and the heart in two separate containers and left them in the van in the parking garage. By the time I was sent the next person, he'd already taken them out of the van."

"I can understand why you murdered Hannah Williams," Harris said. When Langford looked confused, she continued with a shrug. "Yeah, I mean this guy was threatening you, right?

He was the only one who knew you were involved with Lucy's death. He knew you covered it up, and if he exposed you, your life would be over. So, you were willing to do whatever he asked. The letters came, and you figured buying a van and stealing some tools from work were a small price to pay, right?"

Langford sounded like he knew he was being led into a trap. "Yeah."

"And when this guy told you to kill Hannah, you figured you'd be done with it, right? A murder for a murder."

"Where is this going, Detective Harris?" Mr. White asked. He shot her a dirty look, but she wasn't paying attention to him.

"What I want to know is why you kept going. When did you think it would end?"

"He said he needed seven girls," Langford said. "And he assured me that once it was over, I'd never hear from him again."

"And you believed him?"

"Mutually assured destruction."

"Come again?"

Langford leaned forward. "Mutually assured destruction. He knew what I'd done. He took a risk by reaching out to contact me. When I did what he said, I also had something hanging over his head. He knew if I got caught or turned myself in, I'd be able to point in his direction."

"And can you?"

"Can I what?"

"Can you point us in his direction?" Harris crossed her arms. "What do you know about your blackmailer? Do you have any idea who he is?"

"No."

"That's awfully inconvenient for you, Dr. Langford."

"I recognize that." Langford seemed to be keeping his rage in check, marginally. "Trust me, if I could give you a name and an address, I would. But he didn't trust me enough to tell me who he was. Can't say I blame him."

"But you said he picked up the blood and the hearts from the van? Did you ever think to install a camera?"

"Of course, I did." Langford rolled his eyes. "I'm not an idiot. But he found it. Took it. Told me never to try that again or he'd drop an anonymous tip to the police."

"Something isn't lining up here, Dr. Langford."

"Oh yeah? What's that?"

"I think you enjoyed killing those women. I think it started with your girlfriend and snowballed from there. Hell, maybe it started before then. Maybe you were coerced, like you said, but all it took was a little push. You wanted a reason to do it, and you thought you were smart enough to get away with it. Figured you wouldn't get caught. And then, if you did, you could blame it on this so-called blackmailer. With your money, your reputation and a little bit of patience, I'm sure you thought you'd be in and out in no time."

"My client is handing you everything you need to track down his blackmailer," Mr. White said. "A judge and jury of Dr. Langford's peers will be the ones to determine his level of guilt. It's up to you to find the brains of this operation. I suggest you make your moves sooner rather than later."

"You worry about your job, Mr. White, and I'll worry about mine." Harris stared Langford down. "Where will we find these letters?"

"In a safety deposit box in my room. Lucy is buried by the huge oak tree at the edge of my property. You'll see that the only crime I've truly committed is not going to the police after she accidentally fell down the stairs."

"You're guilty of far more than that, Dr. Langford, but lucky for me, you got caught. I know you're not going anywhere, so we'll have plenty of time to prove that later." Harris stood. "I have everything I need for now. Detective Beauregard will take down your statement in full. Do not leave any details out. At this point, leaving details out will hurt you."

Harris didn't wait for a response from Langford. She left the interrogation room and entered the alcove where Cassie, David, the Chief of Police, and the second officer had been watching. She raked her fingers through her ponytail and sat down. All the bluster had gone out of her, and she looked exhausted.

"Excellent job, Harris," the Chief said. "Let the rookies do the leg work now. Get some sleep and we'll put together a plan in the morning."

"Yes, ma'am."

As the Chief and the other officer left, David and Harris turned to Cassie.

"I guess that's it for me," Cassie said. "My job's over."

"Far from it," Harris said. "I don't plan to let you out of my sight until all of this is over. Can't risk you running off again."

"But—"

Harris held up a hand, and David tried to hide his laughter behind a cough. Harris said, "I'll pick you up bright and early tomorrow. Wear some good shoes and eat some bacon and eggs. It's going to be a long day."

32

True to her word, Detective Harris picked Cassie up at eight in the morning. Neither woman felt well-rested. The exhaustion felt like she was walking through molasses every time she took a step forward. She couldn't speak for the detective, but Cassie had trouble falling asleep wondering who Langford's blackmailer could be.

It was someone who wanted seven women dead and their blood drained and their hearts cut out. The blackmailer didn't know any of the women and Cassie was still convinced it was a ritualistic killing. How had the blackmailer picked the women?

It was someone who couldn't or wouldn't kill the women themselves. They were smart enough to drag Langford into the mix and clever enough to know he would be a willing participant. Langford was clear he didn't know who the blackmailer was—and Cassie believed him, or else the doctor would've instantly turned in the blackmailer—but his blackmailer seemed to know the doctor.

Every little noise had kept her up. Was it Elizabeth? Was it the mysterious little boy? She hadn't had any ghostly visitors as far as she knew, but that didn't mean they weren't just out of sight. Not for the first time, Cassie wondered how the spirit world worked and if there was any way she could further tap into it.

She wondered if that was what she wanted. More ghosts? More murders? Wasn't this enough? Hadn't she had enough over the years? These thoughts continued to occupy Cassie's mind all morning.

She and Harris arrived at Langford's house. They hadn't said more than a few words to one another, but Harris seemed to be as lost in thought as Cassie.

When they pulled to a stop, Cassie pushed open her door and looked up at the house.

"Jesus."

"I know," Harris slammed the car door shut behind her. "I got into the wrong profession."

"For real."

The entire house was built out of stone and had a turret in the back. It was two stories, but the square footage was enormous. An array of windows adorned the front from floor to ceiling. It was surrounded by shrubs and trees and gorgeous flowers, all professionally maintained.

"Have you been inside?" Cassie asked.

"Not yet. I wanted to check out where Lucy's body was buried first. They began exhuming her this morning. We should make it in time."

"Perfect," Cassie said. "I love a good exhuming right after breakfast."

"Don't we all."

As the two women walked up the driveway, David met them halfway. He had a coffee in each hand.

"Hello, ladies." He handed over the steaming beverages. "Take these. I'm already at my limit for the day."

"What are you doing here?" Cassie glanced at Harris. "I thought you weren't involved in an official capacity."

"I asked him to be here," Harris said. "And he agreed, despite it being his day off."

David waved off her concern. "Had to file some paperwork because of the, uh, *incident* last night, so I figured I might as well see the job through. Plus, we could use all hands on deck."

"The incident?" Cassie asked. "Is that what we're calling it?"

"Better than Cassie-was-being-a-pain-in-my-ass-again, right?"

"Yeah, yeah."

Harris took a sip of the hot liquid and sighed happily. "So, you know where we're going?"

"Yep. It's about a hundred meters into the woods lining the property over there." David pointed behind the house and off to the right. There was an officer standing at the edge of the trees. "Right by a big oak tree like Langford said."

Cassie glanced around the lot. "Lots of big oaks." She fell in line with the two detectives as they made their way into the trees. "Did Langford say anything else last night? Anything new?"

Harris pushed a branch to the side and waited for Cassie to sidestep it. "No. He gave us most of the basics during the interrogation. His statement was detailed, but no new information. He's sticking to his story."

"I'm surprised his lawyer let him open up like that."

"He didn't have a choice. We caught him in the act. He'll

serve far less time if he owns up to covering Lucy's death and says he was coerced into killing the others."

"Funny how justice works sometimes, isn't it?"

"I wouldn't give up hope yet," David said. "Murder is still murder, even if someone else made him do it, and I don't think there's enough evidence there to show that he was scared for his life. Plus, his obvious lack of remorse. I don't think he's going to be getting out of prison any time soon."

"What about his money? His reputation?" Cassie side-stepped a bramble and continued walking the path David was forging for them. "Do you think that'll give him the upper hand in the courtroom?"

"We'll work to make sure that doesn't happen," Harris didn't sound as confident as Cassie would have liked. "Right now, it's about finding as much evidence as we can to build a clearer picture of what happened."

"What do we know about Lucy?" Cassie asked.

"I had someone reach out to her sister this morning. We have a missing file on Lucy since she's been gone for about two months, but since all evidence pointed to her leaving on her own, there was nothing we could have done about it."

"Sounds like you're still trying to convince yourself of that," Cassie said.

"It's hard," Harris replied. "You do the best you can, but it's not always enough. You're going to miss something and you're going to make mistakes. If we had known about Lucy earlier, maybe we could've saved Sage or Elizabeth. But that wasn't in the cards for us."

"And we did save Katie and hopefully whoever he had planned for victims six and seven."

"You were almost number six," Harris said.

Cassie inhaled and held it for an extra beat. "No, I was bonus number one. Six and seven are still out there."

"Five, too." Harris scratched the back of her head. "Lucy was how Langford had described her, as far as we can tell. She was a good person. Did some charity work and kept her head down. Not even a parking ticket. She was way too good for that jerk. She didn't deserve to go out the way she did, accident or not."

"They rarely do," said Cassie.

The three of them fell silent and Cassie allowed herself to tune into the woods around her. It felt normal on the surface—full of birds and bugs and deer and squirrels—but beneath that, she felt the chill of the spirit world. She was doubtful that Lucy's body was the only one buried here. She felt an overwhelming sensation that took over when she felt she wasn't doing enough, but David's words from last night came back to her.

You can't save everyone.

She wished she could. It would make the world a better place. But David was right. Finding Lucy's body and helping the women Langford had killed find peace would have to be enough. And after that, she would try to help the next victim. If she could.

She always believed having a future laid out for herself was the best path forward, but her experience with Novak proved anything could happen, regardless of plans.

Maybe the right move was just putting one foot in front of the other. Having a plan was good, but there had to be wiggle room for the obstacles that might pop up. Life had a habit of throwing curve balls, after all.

"It's up ahead," David said. "Come on."

Cassie followed his footsteps until they reached the large

oak tree. Spanish moss swung in the gentle breeze. She caught the faint smell of eucalyptus and searched the woods for the telltale velvet bark but spotted none.

There were several other officers waiting for them. A lumpy figure under a not-so white sheet was lying next to a hole at the base of the tree. When one of the officers spotted the group approaching, he jogged over to Harris.

"Morning, Detective. We're just finishing up. Shouldn't take much longer." His eyes moved past her and landed on Cassie. "Ma'am."

Cassie nodded.

"This is Ms. Quinn," David said. "She's consulting with us on the case."

The officer nodded and turned his gaze back to Harris. "We've done our initial sweep. Nothing else in the area but tread light if you can. It's rained enough times that there's no footprints or anything. But we'd like to do another final look or two before we do an official wrap-up."

"Sounds good. Thank you." Harris turned to Cassie. "You ready for this?"

"No, but let's do it anyway," Cassie said.

Harris gave her a tight smile and nodded. She had already switched on the detective persona and Cassie didn't want to get in the way. She was there to observe. There were things that only she might see.

"As far as we can tell, Langford has been truthful with us," David said. He brought the pair of them to the body. "Lucy was buried here, under the tree, like he said."

"What do we know about the body so far?"

The officer who had greeted them knelt and looked at Harris, then at Cassie, then back at Harris. When the detective nodded her head, he slipped the sheet off Lucy. "Normal decomposition as far as we can tell. We'll need to do a tox screen and all that, but it's clear her neck was broken. So far, everything lines up."

"Langford doesn't have a reason to lie," David said, stroking his chin. "If he gets pinned for this murder, it'll reinforce the story he told us about the blackmail."

A chill ran down Cassie's spine and she let David's words fade away. When she turned, she saw a figure standing next to the large oak. She didn't know what Lucy looked like in life, but given the odd angle of the spirit's neck, Cassie was certain it was her.

Cassie saw ghosts when they were at their most vulnerable or terrified. Rarely did she get to see that moment when they found peace, but it was clear from Lucy's face she was finding her peace. She kept eye contact with Cassie as a single tear rolled down her face. She smiled, though it was tight, and faded from view.

There was no bright light and Cassie didn't see her spirit fly into the sky, but a feeling in the pit of her stomach told her that Lucy moved on to wherever they went after they found peace. Her body had been discovered and the truth about her death was known. For Lucy, that seemed to be enough.

"Cassie? Cassie?" David took a step closer. "Are you okay?"

Cassie started and turned toward him. The smile on her face was genuine. "Yeah, I'm good."

"Are you ready to go inside?"

"I'm ready," she said. "Let's go."

33

David, Harris, and Cassie emerged from the woods. Halfway across the lawn, Cassie felt the shift in Harris's mood. It was like a shadow had fallen across their little group, cold and dark and heavy with foreboding.

"What the hell is she doing here?"

Cassie followed the detective's gaze and saw Ms. Campbell, the reporter, pulling up the driveway in a news van. Her cameraman was driving, and Campbell's blonde curls bounced every time the vehicle hit a bump.

A police officer emerged from the house and ran over to the vehicle before it even stopped and approached the reporter's window.

"Hey, I recognize that guy," Cassie tried to keep up with the long strides of David and Harris.

"Who, Ramirez?"

"I don't remember his name, but he's the one who took my statement," she said. "He was also at the crime scene."

Harris pulled up short. "What crime scene?"

"The one where she showed up," Cassie pointed to Ms. Campbell. "Sage's crime scene. They had words when your back was turned, and he gave her a death glare the entire time she was there."

Harris didn't say anything. She resumed her march across the lawn, and David and Cassie struggled to keep pace. When Officer Ramirez saw her coming, he backed off and tried to return to the house.

"Ramirez, hang on a minute." Harris pointed to the cameraman about to get out of his car. "You stay there. Don't you dare move."

"Detective Harris, the people have a right to—"

Harris cut him off. "You're on private property," Harris interrupted. "And you're interrupting an active police investigation."

"Is the owner of this house a suspect?"

Harris ignored the reporter and turned to Ramirez. "How do you know Ms. Campbell?"

The man stuttered over his words and nothing came out. The reporter was quiet.

"I will find out one way or another, so you might as well come clean and save some of your dignity in the process."

"We're dating." Ramirez turned to Ms. Campbell and gave her a withering look. "*Were* dating."

The reporter looked scandalized. "Are you serious?"

It was Ramirez's turn to ignore her. "Detective Harris, I swear I didn't do any of this on purpose. I was worried about her. She's always going out on her own trying to get a story and I wanted to scare her."

"What did you tell her?" Harris placed herself in front of Campbell so Ramirez couldn't look to her for suggestions.

Ramirez ran a hand down his face. "I told her the killer was cutting women open and pulling their hearts out of their chests. She promised not to say anything."

"She lied."

"I was trying to keep her safe." Ramirez looked back over at his girlfriend with a pained look on his face. "And she used me."

Ms. Campbell reached for him. "Charlie—"

Ramirez turned his back on her. "I think she's been using the Find My Phone feature to track where I'm going during the day. That's why she showed up to the last crime scene before anyone else. And how she figured out where I was today." Ramirez took a huge gulp of air. His face darkened. "I swear, I had no idea until today."

"David, do you mind checking Ramirez's phone? Send one of the other officers back to the precinct with him. Let the Chief know. We'll see how she wants to handle it."

Ramirez hung his head and followed David back to the house, handing his phone over in the process.

Harris turned her attention back to the reporter. Her cameraman was still half out of the van, but he kept a steady gaze on the detective. He didn't dare move until she gave him permission.

"Is all of that true?" Harris asked.

"More or less." Campbell didn't sound remorseful. "It's not a crime to do my job."

"It's a crime to do your job poorly," Harris said. "And it's definitely a crime to go through someone else's phone and track them when that person is a police officer working on a highly-sensitive case."

Ms. Campbell looked over at her cameraman who shrugged his shoulders.

"Let the record show that I could make your life a living hell," Harris continued. "Your boss, Mr. Sinclair? He and my father were pretty good friends back in the day. I guarantee you that Bill is more worried about staying on my good side than he is about staying on yours."

For the first time, Campbell looked worried. "I was trying—"

"To do your job? Yes. I know." Harris put her hands on her hips. "I'm going to give you some insider information, off the record. And it will stay off the record, do you understand?"

"Yes, ma'am."

"That stunt you pulled the other day. You know, when you released information about how those women were killed, you remember that?"

Campbell's jaw was set. "Yes, ma'am."

"That was sensitive information that we could've used to corner a suspect. But since you chose to make it public knowledge, you took one of our tools away. It could've been your fault that we might've missed out on catching this guy."

"I—"

"I'm not done." Harris took a step forward and Cassie saw the reporter shrink back. "This is the part that stays off the record. Do you understand?"

"Yes, ma'am."

"This isn't over yet and if you report on what you saw here today, you will, without a doubt, be charged as an accessory. Am I clear?"

The reporter gulped. "Crystal, ma'am."

Harris turned to the cameraman. "That goes for you, too."

"Yes, ma'am." His voice cracked halfway through.

"Get in your van, drive away, and go home. I will be calling your boss to let him know you crossed the line, but that I am interested in giving you an exclusive when this is over."

"An exclusive? Why would you do that?"

"It's a peace offering," Harris said. "I don't need enemies in the media, and something tells me you're going to be around for a while. If you can sit tight for a few more days, I promise I'll give you a story worth telling."

"I appreciate that, Detective."

Harris looked at the reporter for a long moment. "Can I give you a word of advice, Ms. Campbell?" When she nodded, Harris continued. "You'll catch more flies with honey than vinegar."

"I've heard that."

"That doesn't surprise me. You're good at your job. I think you have a promising career ahead of you. You're going to make enemies throughout your life. Make sure it's worth the trouble."

Campbell nodded her head and got back into the van. Her cameraman slammed his own door shut and performed a K turn and drove back the way they came.

Cassie waved her hand in front of her face to clear the exhaust and dirt that kicked up in the van's wake. "Do you think that'll work?"

"For a while, maybe." Harris watched them go. "But not forever. She's smart. She's tough. She'll do what she needs to in order to get a story. If she sees me as a willing source, she'll behave."

"How hard was it not to cuff her just to see the look on her face?"

Harris threw her head back, laughing. "So hard! I thought about doing it, like, three times."

The pair of them turned back to the house. "What are you going to do with Ramirez?" Cassie asked.

"I don't know. I kind of hope Chief goes easy on him. I don't think he had any idea. But there needs to be consequences to his actions, otherwise he'll keep making mistakes."

Cassie opened her mouth to agree with Detective Harris, but movement out of the corner of her eye made her turn as she was about to step through the entrance to Langford's house. It took her a moment to figure out what she was looking at, but as soon as she did, a lump formed in her throat.

The ghost of the little boy who had spent months standing in the corner of her bedroom stood at the corner of the house, staring at her as though he had a million things to say.

But before Cassie could comprehend what was going on, her phone buzzed in her pocket. When she pulled it out, she had no idea who she expected the caller to be, but she wasn't prepared to see her sister Laura calling her for the first time in months.

And by the time she looked back up, the boy's figure vanished into the ether.

34

"Cassie, you ready to go?"

Harris was impatient, and it took Cassie's brain a minute to catch up with everything that was going on. She was experiencing sensory overload.

"My sister's calling." Cassie held up her phone as evidence. "She doesn't call unless it's an emergency. Can I meet you inside?"

"Make it quick," Harris said.

Cassie nodded and hit the answer button on her phone. "Hello?"

Her sister's laughter filled the other end of the line, but it sounded off. "Why do you sound like you don't know who's calling you? Doesn't your phone have caller ID?"

"Yes." Cassie rolled her eyes and started walking to the corner of the house where she had seen the little boy's ghost. "I wasn't expecting a call from you. Is everything okay?"

"That's how you know we don't talk enough," Laura said. "Why does something have to be wrong?"

Cassie could still tell this wasn't a normal phone call, but she decided to play along. "You're right. I'm sorry. How are you?"

"Pretty good, all things considered. California is *so* expensive."

Cassie laughed. "You say that every time."

"And I'll keep saying it until it's not."

"Good luck with that one," Cassie said. She searched the phone for something—anything—that she could pull from her memory about what was going on in her sister's life. "Are you still seeing Alan?"

Laura sighed heavily. "No. He was a good guy, but boring as all hell."

"Boring is good sometimes. Don't take it for granted."

"I'm saving boring for my thirties, like you. I want fun and excitement!"

"Just not too much fun and excitement."

"Of course, *you* would say that." Laura's tone rolled her eyes for her. "What about you? Are you leading a boring life?"

"Never." Cassie laughed at the idea. She had been dreaming about a boring life for a while, but the concept was too far-fetched. "But the museum's going well."

"Still helping the police with their investigations?"

Cassie sighed. Her sister knew more than her parents did, but she didn't know the complete story. As far as Laura knew, she was a bit of an amateur detective. Cassie wasn't sure if Laura thought it was because of her run-ins with Novak or because she had a strange talent for solving murders. Either way, Cassie was sure her sister had no idea the spirit world was involved.

"Yeah," Cassie said. She rounded the corner of the house but was disappointed when all she saw was open air. Had the little boy disappeared, or was he playing hide-and-go-seek? "I'm at a crime scene as we speak."

"Oh, really? That's not boring."

"No, it's not." Cassie weighed her next words. "I know you called for a reason."

Laura sighed. "I don't want to interrupt you if you're working."

"Working? You know they don't pay me for this, right?"

Laura laughed. "You should maybe look into getting compensated."

"I'll do that. Now stop stalling. What's up?"

The silence stretched on and Cassie could hear the gears turning in her sister's head. "Look, there's no easy way to say this, so I'm going to be blunt about it. Mom's sick."

Cassie felt dizzy and had to put a hand on the side of the house to steady herself. "What?"

"She found out a couple months ago, I guess. She made dad keep it secret, but I don't think he could anymore. He told me and begged me not to tell you, but I can't keep something like this quiet. What are they thinking?"

"Why didn't she want to tell us?"

"You know Mom," Laura said. "She doesn't want to bother anyone."

"Jesus Christ. She'd wait until we surrounded her on her death bed to tell us she's dying."

"Probably."

"Is it bad?"

"She has a brain tumor."

"You're shitting me."

Laura laughed. "Wish I was. She said she started to feel pressure behind her eyes that wouldn't go away. Had some trouble seeing. She knew something was off, so she got checked out."

Cassie's entire body got hot. "Is she going to be okay? Are they worried?"

"They checked her out, and it doesn't look like it spread anywhere else. They'll need to do a biopsy to be sure, but it's nothing to get worked up about."

"Those sound like dad's words."

"Funny how he had to call me because he was worried but spent the next hour saying it wasn't a big deal."

"Parents are weird that way." Cassie took a deep breath. "So, she'll need brain surgery?"

"I guess so." There was the hint of a tremor in Laura's voice. "They have a couple more appointments to go to before they set up the big surgery, so they'll have to get through those first."

Cassie hesitated to say what was on her mind, but she had to ask. "Why didn't I get a phone call?"

Laura blew a big breath into the phone's mic. "I don't know, Cass. I really don't. Things have been strained between all of us."

"I'm sorry—"

"I know you are. It sucked when you pushed us all away, but I get it. You went through all that trauma. I'm always going to love you, and I'm always going to be there for you, even if you don't want me to be."

Tears filled Cassie's eyes and she sniffled. "Thank you. I want you in my life. You're my sister."

"You're welcome," Laura said. "But you have to do more than that."

"Me? What do you mean?"

"It's time to apologize to Mom and Dad. It's time to repair things."

"I'm not the only one—"

"I know that, Cassie. I know. But listen, they dropped everything for you, and you were a good sport for a while—"

"A good sport?"

Laura kept going as if she hadn't been interrupted. "But you kicked them out of your life. You kicked all of us out. We've all been hanging by threads for the last couple years, and I'm tired of it. I want my family back."

"I didn't go anywhere."

"Yes, you did. And I get it. You've been through so much, and that takes a lot of time to heal. A lot longer than a few years."

"Are you using your psych degree on me?"

"So what if I am?" Laura laughed, her voice still quivering. "Cassie, I think you've come a long way in the last ten years. From the few conversations we've had, I think you've done a lot of healing. But you won't be able to close those wounds until you talk to Mom and Dad."

"What about you?"

"Me too, if you can squeeze me in."

"Yeah, I can." Cassie gasped. "Is this an intervention?"

"Definitely not." Laura's laugh was stronger. "Mom and Dad have their own issues to sort through, too. They spent a long time keeping us as close as possible. I had to move to California to grow up. You had to almost die. Twice."

"Thanks for reminding me."

"The point is, I think we need to go home."

"That sounds terrifying. But--" Cassie said, "--I want to see

221

mom. I want to make sure everything is okay. I do want to fix this, Laura."

"Good. Me too." The sound of rustling papers filled the phone for a minute. "My next appointment will be here soon, but do me a favor? Look at your calendar. Let me know when you can get away for a week. I'll fly into Savannah and we can have some sister time before we head to Charlotte."

"You know, I'm the big sister," Cassie said. "You're way too mature right now."

"We all have to grow up some time," Laura said. "But if it makes you feel better, I'll let you be in charge when we're around Mom and Dad."

"Gee, thanks."

"Hey," Laura said. "I love you."

Cassie's throat tightened with emotion and she recalled the hands wrapped around it less than twenty-four hours prior. "I love you, too."

"Call me soon, okay? Promise me?"

"I promise. Thanks for calling me."

"You're welcome. Bye, sis."

"Bye."

Cassie hung up the phone and was consumed with a well of emotion. While Laura had sounded casual about their mother's prognosis, it was not easy to hear that kind of news. The idea of reuniting with her family was terrifying, but Laura had a point. They couldn't stay like this forever. They'd have to talk about their problems one day.

But the major question was whether Cassie would ever feel comfortable confiding in them about her abilities. They wouldn't try to lock her up in an insane asylum, but she also didn't want to make matters worse.

Only time would tell.

Cassie looked around one more time and headed back to the front of the house. She couldn't see the ghost of the little boy anywhere. Why had he shown up now? Why here? It was the first time she had seen him out of her house and it didn't make sense. Langford was a killer, but so far, his entire demographic of victims was grown women. The little boy didn't belong.

Cassie reached the front of the house and met David at the entrance.

"Everything okay?" he asked.

"My mother has a brain tumor." Cassie's casual tone surprised herself. "I think I'm still processing it, but my sister said they don't think it's cancer. We'll have to wait until it's removed to find out."

"I'm so sorry." David's face was a mask of concern. "Is there anything I can do?"

"Let's solve one problem at a time," she said. "I could use the distraction."

35

The inside of Langford's house was more impressive than the outside, but Cassie didn't have much time to look around. It was big and open and somehow devoid of any real personality. It wasn't that she wouldn't be happy to live in a house of this size, but a home needed some warmth and a welcoming atmosphere. This one felt sterile.

She followed David up the stairs and tried to not think about the fact that this was where Lucy had lost her life. She focused on the task ahead of them.

Harris met them at the door. "Everything okay?"

"Some personal stuff. Nothing I can do about it now." Cassie looked over Harris's shoulder. "Did you find the letters?"

"Right where he told us they'd be." Harris stepped to the side.

Cassie's breath caught in her throat. Langford's bedroom was at least three times the size of her own. He fit a king bed, two dressers, a TV cabinet, and several bookshelves in there, and it still felt open and airy. Comfortable.

And she had been right about the floor-to-ceiling windows.

"Impressive, right?" David asked. "Why do terrible people always have the best stuff?"

Cassie shrugged. She had been wondering the same thing. Langford was a doctor, and it was clear that he either made good money or came from a wealthy family. Maybe both. She didn't know how much a house like this cost, but she knew it wasn't cheap.

"Why would he risk losing any of this?" Cassie wondered. "I mean, I know money isn't everything, but was he so bored with his life that he thought he'd spend some time murdering people?"

"It doesn't always make sense," Harris said. "And you'll drive yourself crazy asking why."

"She's right," David said. "We have to be satisfied that we caught him. The next step is to make sure he goes to prison for a very long time."

"Actually," Harris said. "The next step is finding out who his blackmailer is."

Cassie walked over to Langford's bed and looked at the letters spread out across the top of it. There were at least a dozen of them, and they all looked ordinary. It was strange to think they had been used to instruct Langford in committing such horrific crimes.

"Okay." Cassie blew out a breath. "What are we working with?"

Harris handed Cassie a pair of gloves. "So far, everything adds up. We've put them in chronological order as best as we could according to what Langford told us and using our best judgment. It starts with the initial requests, then goes into the letters about the women."

"May I?" David looked at Harris.

"Go ahead."

"What I found interesting is that whoever wrote these letters was familiar with Dr. Langford. He called him by his first name, Richard, and used phrases that implied they must've crossed paths at some point."

"So, Langford does know who the blackmailer is?" Cassie asked.

"Not necessarily." David leaned forward and used a gloved hand to point out a couple lines here and there. "The blackmailer says things like '*I know it won't be hard for you to take a life, given that your profession deals in death every day,*' or this one that says '*Your competency and willingness to take risks is what drew me to you.*'"

"Maybe he was a patient?" Cassie asked. "Is that possible?"

"Anything's possible at this point," Harris said, "but yes, it seems like the blackmailer could be one of Langford's patients or someone who was aware of him."

"And that's why they chose Langford? Because Langford was smart enough to get away with murder and cavalier enough to not care that he was playing with people's lives?"

"Seems like it." Harris pointed to the first letter. "In this one he talks about seeing the newspaper article describing Lucy's disappearance. He put two and two together and figured it out. He said Langford was too smart for the police, but not smart enough to outplay him."

Cassie groaned. "Great, another arrogant jerk."

"On the plus side, this guy likes to talk. Some of these letters are three or four pages long. That means we'll be able to get more information from them."

"You mean he didn't sign his name at the bottom? That's rude."

"I miss the days when serial killers told us who they were," David said.

"Luckily," Harris interrupted, "we can tell a few other things from the letters."

"For one," David continued, "the paper."

"It looks normal to me," Cassie said, leaning closer.

"Every detail is important. It's stationery paper, not ordinary computer paper. There are no lines on it and no logos, watermarks or designs, either."

"Also inconvenient," Cassie said.

David ignored her. "This could be his personal stationary or he might've bought it for this purpose. Either way, I doubt we'll be able to track him down from the type of paper he chose."

"So, it gave us no information?"

"I wouldn't say that," Harris said. "Sometimes the absence of information is useful, too. It helps us rule out other factors."

"Fair enough," Cassie said. "What else?"

"He used black ink," David continued. "We'll be able to analyze that. But again, I doubt we'll be able to track him down based on the type of pen he used."

"He wrote in cursive, though," Harris said. "His handwriting is nice and neat."

"Rules out another doctor," Cassie said. When Harris and David looked confused, she shrugged. "Their handwriting is always terrible."

"Still, younger generations weren't beaten over the head with cursive the way some of us older folks were. The way he's formed some of these letters, he might be older. Or went to a private school."

Cassie looked up at David to see if he was joking. His face was serious. "You can tell all of that from his handwriting?"

"Yes and no." David stood up and stretched his back. "These are educated guesses, emphasis on the guess. What will help is if we can pull any fingerprints off the paper."

"What's the likelihood of that?" Cassie asked.

Harris shrugged. "This guy seems smart. Don't think he would make a mistake like that, but maybe he overestimated Langford. Maybe he figured Langford wouldn't get caught, and therefore the letters would never be found."

Cassie looked back down at the letters in front of her. She had avoided looking too closely, but her eyes were drawn to Elizabeth's letter. The picture was taken from Facebook or a dating profile. It was pixelated, but that did not distort how happy she was.

Cassie was overcome with immense sadness. For the detectives, the victims were already dead and gone. Their stories were over, and it was time to give them justice. But for Cassie, there was more to it. Elizabeth wasn't gone and neither were the other three victims. Their souls hadn't been laid to rest. Their mystery hadn't been solved.

Cassie reached for Elizabeth's letter, hesitated, and looked up at Harris. "My turn?"

Harris gestured toward the letter.

Cassie turned her attention back to the paper and as soon as she made contact, she felt a tingling surge in the tips of her fingers. She snatched her hand back, but the vision had already taken hold of her.

Unlike the vision Jessica had given her, Cassie wasn't transported to another place and time. She was aware of being in Langford's bedroom surrounded by David, Harris, and the other police officers. But a series of images flashed in her mind. She swayed on her feet as she tried to make sense of it.

"Cassie?" David asked, his voice tinged with worry. "Are you okay? Did you see something?"

"A basement," Cassie said. The image was already fading, and she was trying to hold onto it. "With an altar."

"What?" Harris asked. "What's happ—"

"What else?" David had witnessed this on more than one occasion. "Come on, talk to me."

Cassie turned to him and shook her head. "It went by so fast."

"Describe anything you can."

"It was dark. Almost pitch black. But there were candles lit on a small table. Some weird symbols drawn on the wall behind it."

"Could you see any identifying markers? Could you tell what kind of house it was?"

"It went by so fast."

"Do you want to try again?"

Cassie nodded and reached for another letter. She hesitated for a fraction of a second before making contact, but once she did, nothing happened. There was no electric buzz, no dizziness, and no flashing images.

Cassie touched another letter, and another. She touched every single letter about each of the victims and then moved to the others. When she looked back at David, he already knew what she had found.

"Nothing," he said.

"I'm sorry," Harris said, holding out her hands, "but what just happened?"

"Sometimes I get flashes," Cassie said.

"Flashes?" Harris looked dubious. "Of what?"

"Images. Sometimes like a cut scene." Cassie was still trying to recall the picture, but with every passing minute it became darker and darker, like it was fading from her memory at lightning speed. "I'm assuming the basement belongs to the blackmailer, but I can't be sure." Harris shot David a look and he left the room only to reappear a minute later. Harris raised an inquisitive eyebrow when he reentered.

"No basement," he said. "Didn't figure there would be in this part of town being at sea level and all."

"I thought so. We're back to the blackmailer then," Harris said. "But that description isn't going to get us far."

"I know. I'm sorry."

Harris took a deep breath. "It's okay. We need to get these to the lab anyway. Let's go back to the precinct and regroup. Maybe something will come to you on the way."

"Sounds like a plan," Cassie said, knowing it was a longshot.

36

David held the door open for Cassie and Detective Harris and shuffled in behind them. The entrance to the precinct was more active than usual. There was a man and a woman arguing loudly off to the side, while another man spoke to the intake officer. When the woman at the front desk caught sight of the three of them walking in, she sighed with relief.

"Detective Harris," her voice carried over the screaming couple. "I was about to call you."

"Everything okay?"

The woman pointed to the man standing in front of her. "Other than Savannah going crazy like there's a full moon tonight, this gentleman has information relevant to your case."

Harris stepped up to the man at the counter. "What can I do for you?"

The man turned and took her hand. Cassie thought he looked a bit like Langford. He was tall and trim with wide shoulders and a strong jaw. The difference was in their eyes.

This man looked kind. He looked like he cared. And he looked like he had something he had to get off his chest.

"My name is Bradley Baker, and I think I know who the killer is."

The entranceway fell silent. The couple stopped yelling and were staring at the group with unabashed interest. David was the first to regain his composure.

"Let's take this somewhere more private, shall we?"

Bradley nodded and the four made their way toward the back of the precinct to one of the more spacious meeting rooms. Harris pulled out a chair for Bradley and sat across from him.

Cassie wasn't sure what to do. "Should I go, or—"

"Sit," Harris said. "Stay, please."

"I'll grab us some waters." David backed out of the room.

"Mr. Baker, was it?" Harris asked.

"Doctor," Baker said, shifting in his seat. "Dr. Baker. Call me Bradley."

"My name is Adelaide," Harris said. "And this is Cassie."

Bradley looked between the two of them and smiled. "You must think I'm nuts."

"Not at all," Harris said. "But I will say we already have a suspect in custody."

"Is it Langford?" Bradley sat up straighter when he saw the shock on Harris's face. "I knew it. Jesus Christ. I knew it. I should've said something sooner."

"Whoa, whoa, hang on," Harris said. "Let's start at the beginning, okay?"

David returned with the waters and set them in the middle of the table and retreated to the corner of the room and leaning against the wall.

"The beginning," Bradley said. "Okay. Well, I work with Dr. Richard Langford at Candler Hospital. I didn't know him in school, but we started at Candler at the same time. We've worked together for, uh, some years. I'm sorry, I can't—I can't remember how long."

"It's okay," Harris said. "Take a deep breath. Drink some water. There's no rush here, okay? Get through it in your own time."

Bradley nodded and grabbed one of the water bottles. This new side of Harris surprised Cassie. She was calm and compassionate. This was the side she showed when she talked to victims and their families. The side of her that cared about people. The side that remembered why she did this job in the first place.

Bradley drank half the bottle of water. He screwed the top back on and placed it on the table. "Richard Langford and I have known each other for, oh, I'd say, six or seven years. I wouldn't call us friends, but there's no outward animosity between us. We didn't socialize, and if we had to work together, we kept it professional."

"Sounds like a decent work colleague," Harris encouraged.

"I've had worse." Bradley laughed, but not for long. "Langford can be a bit of a dick, to be honest. I learned to steer clear of him and he left me alone. I know he was cheating on his girlfriend with a couple different nurses at the hospital."

"Did you know his girlfriend?"

"I'd seen her at the hospital a couple of times. She'd bring him dinner once in a while when we worked late. She seemed sweet, but we never talked. Langford complained about her all the time, but I took it with a grain of salt. I doubted half of what he said was true. The rest of it was probably blown out of proportion. And one day, I noticed she had disappeared."

"Did that surprise you?" Harris asked.

Bradley shook his head. "Not really. He played the part for a couple days but seemed to get over it rather quickly. It didn't sit right with me, but people grieve in their own way. And I hoped maybe she dropped him, you know? Got out of a bad situation."

Harris's eyebrows knit together. "According to Langford, they got into a fight and she fell down the stairs. He covered up the accident and made it look like she left town."

"Oh." Bradley stared at an imaginary spot on the conference table. "That's too bad. She seemed sweet."

"Correct me if I'm wrong," Harris continued, her voice gentle, "but I don't think you're here to talk about Lucy, are you?"

Bradley cleared his throat and took another drink of water. "No. About a month ago, I noticed he was distracted. He's a good doctor, but his bedside manner has always sucked. He went off on a couple of patients and a few nurses, but nothing major. Most people figured he was still grieving."

"But not you?"

"He stole some things from the hospital," Bradley said. "One of them was a bone saw. I saw him take it. I didn't think much about it at the time. I thought maybe he was selling tools on the side. Like, maybe he had gotten in with some bad people and he was doing anything he could to make extra money."

"That could've explained his girlfriend's disappearance, too," Harris offered.

"I didn't know for sure." Bradley's eyes were wide. "I didn't have any evidence and I didn't want to accuse him—"

"No one's blaming you. You couldn't have known. You

didn't do anything wrong." Harris waited until Bradley nodded reluctantly. "What made you recall the bone saw?"

"The news," Bradley said. "Something wasn't adding up. I looked at his schedule and noticed he had one of the nurses move his shifts around. For all four murders, he wasn't working the previous night. He was off every single time."

"You did the right thing coming to us," Harris said. "And I hope you can take some comfort in knowing that you were right. We caught Langford in the act and he's in custody."

"Good." Bradley swallowed hard. "Good."

The silence stretched on until David was the one to break it. "Why don't you seem reassured?"

Bradley took another large gulp of water. "Well, see, I don't think he was working alone."

Cassie and David exchanged looks, but Harris kept her eyes on the man across from her. "Why's that?"

"Because." Bradley looked at each one of them, redirecting to Detective Harris. "My father, William Baker, had something to do with it, too."

37

The room was dead silent for a solid thirty seconds. Harris sat up and placed her hands on the table. She seemed almost too calm for the current situation.

"What makes you say that?" Harris sounded stern.

Bradley took a deep breath, held it for the count of three, and let it out in one large rush. "My father and I aren't close, but we do see each other about once a month or so and have for the last three years. Ever since he had his first heart attack."

Cassie couldn't help the little "oh" that escaped her mouth.

"Yeah." Bradley ran a hand through his hair. "Look, this is going to sound nuts—"

"It won't." Harris glanced at Cassie. "Trust me when I say this case has challenged my own perception of reality. I'll give anything a chance at this point. Tell us your story and we'll figure out what it all means in the end, okay?"

"My father and I aren't close," Bradley repeated. "We never have been. He's the stereotypical man's man and I was always more sensitive than he wanted me to be. As soon as I turned 18, I left home and decided to become a doctor. I think it was the first time he was proud of me. Of course, I saw being a doctor as a way to help people. He saw it as a path to earn respect and wield power. But I didn't care about power. I wanted to travel the world and cure people in remote villages. Help the people who were always overlooked."

"That sounds like a good dream to follow," Harris offered.

Bradley's smile was tight. "Well, my father didn't think so. He thought it was a waste of time. He wanted me to work in New York City and earn loads of money. He didn't want me to waste my inheritance on people he thought would be better off dead anyway."

"So, you had a falling out?"

"For about eight years," Bradley said. "Then three years ago, he had his first heart attack. My parents are divorced but my mom is still his beneficiary. They called her when he was in the hospital and of course, she called me. I visited him a few times, but it was hard. He couldn't understand why he was having a heart attack. He was healthy. Athletic, even. Not pushing seventy yet. I tried to tell him that sometimes that's how the dice are rolled. Genetics could play a huge part in it."

"How did he take that?"

"Not well." Bradley laughed, but it was cold. "He went crazy. Went through doctors like candy. If one wouldn't give him what he wanted, he found another. Started getting into holistic medicine. He started looking...elsewhere."

"Elsewhere?" Harris asked.

Cassie's skin pricked.

"My dad inherited a lot of money when my grandfather died. After my parents divorced, my dad went off the deep end.

Became a recluse. I don't know how he lived when I wasn't talking to him, but it wouldn't take a doctor to see that something was off about him. It got worse after he had his first couple heart attacks. He started taking flights all around the world, looking for anyone who could cure him."

"Correct me if I'm wrong," David interrupted, "but modern medicine can do wonders these days. Having a heart attack today isn't like having one fifty years ago."

"You're right," Bradley said. "We have devices that'll regulate your heartbeat. We can put in stents to help keep arteries open. Hell, we can take a healthy heart out of a person who's passed on and put it in a different person."

"But none of that was good enough for your father?" David asked.

"Apparently not. He wanted a cure, not a temporary fix. He kept having heart attacks and doctors kept saving his life. But every time he walked out of the hospital, he'd start ranting and raving about finding a way to live forever."

"Immortality?" Harris couldn't hide the disbelief in her voice.

"Look, I know how it sounds." Bradley ran a hand down his face. "Trust me, I know. He sounds crazy. He *is* crazy."

"Why do you think he's behind these murders?"

"About a year ago, Dad started inviting me out to dinner once a month. I didn't want to go, but Mom said it would be good for him. Maybe good for me, too. He wouldn't live forever, despite him saying otherwise and she thought it would be a good idea to bury the hatchet and make peace with him while I could."

"Your mom sounds like a good person."

"One of the best," Bradley said. He smiled, but after a few

seconds, it faded. "Dad told me about going to India and finding some shaman or priestess or something that told him how he could fix his heart. How he could cure himself. I don't pretend to know everything and there's a lot of ancient forms of medicine that we're still trying to understand to this day, but I've seen the kinds of people he was describing. Some of them are con artists. If you pay them enough money, they'll tell you a very convincing lie and by the time you figure out you've been duped, your pockets are a lot lighter."

"Did you tell your father this?" Harris asked.

"It didn't go over well." He rolled his eyes. "We had another fight, and I didn't talk to him for another two months. But then he reached out again, said he wanted to go to dinner. I figured he was trying in his own way and I figured I should try, too."

"Did he talk to you about the shaman again?"

"He didn't bring it up. Things were normal for a while."

"Until?"

"Until he started asking about Langford."

Harris sat up straighter. "How did he know about Langford?"

"I'd talked about him over dinner on more than one occasion. For a while I couldn't figure out what to talk about, so I talked about work. A lot of weird stuff happens in a hospital, a lot of funny things. I complained about Langford's arrogance, about how I didn't think he cared about people. At first my dad's questions about him were normal. I could tell he was trying to engage, you know? And later, the questions got rather specific."

"Specific how?"

"He'd ask what I thought about his technique as a surgeon. If he was skilled or not. He'd ask if he'd ever done heart surgery. I thought maybe he was looking for a recommendation for a new doctor, so I answered all his questions."

"When did you realize that's not why he was asking?"

"It took me too long." Bradley's gaze drifted between them, a thousand-yard stare in a hundred-fifty-square-foot room. "Way too long."

Harris reached out and put a gentle hand on Bradley's arm. "Hey, you couldn't have known, okay? About either one of them. Nobody suspects that of the people in their lives. But you're doing the right thing about talking to us now."

"I didn't put two and two together until a few days ago." Bradley was angry with himself despite Harris's words. "Something clicked. I thought back to what he'd said about the shaman. I investigated places he'd gone and did some searching online. There are a lot of articles out there about modern ritualistic sacrifices. Human sacrifices. They believe in this eye for an eye thing. Is your kid sick? Kill another kid and bury them under your house. Your kid will get better. And if he doesn't, you performed the ritual wrong."

"Bradley, I believe you—" Harris started.

"But?" he said.

"But we need evidence. I need to be able to issue an arrest warrant for him."

"I don't have anything," Bradley said. "I wish I did, but—"

"Handwriting," Cassie spoke for the first time in what felt like hours. "Would you recognize your father's handwriting?"

"Uh, sure, I think so. Why?"

"On it." David rushed out of the room. A moment later, he came back with a few different letters and laid them out in front of Bradley. But David didn't come back *alone*.

Elizabeth was right behind him.

Cassie closed her eyes and took a deep breath. When she opened them again, Elizabeth was standing in the corner of the room as a silent observer. Cassie wanted to tell David that Elizabeth was there, but with Bradley in the room, she didn't dare.

Cassie looked down at the letters on the table. She didn't recognize two of them, but Harris gestured to all three.

"Okay, Bradley. We're going to do this on the fly because we don't have much time. This is so we can convince a judge to give us a warrant to search your dad's property." David pulled three letters from evidence. One of them was written by the blackmailer. "Can you tell me with any certainty, which one—"

"This one." Bradley pointed to the blackmailer's letters. "He wrote out a lot of notes when he was being treated. He used to have me read through what all the doctors told him to see if any of them were lying or trying to take advantage of him. It's this one."

"That's good enough for me," David said.

Harris nodded her head. "Then it's good enough for me, too."

38

The intensity level in the precinct increased a thousandfold. The air, no longer stale, rushed past, carrying the smell of early fall through the building every time someone opened an exterior door.

Harris handed Bradley over to Detective Beauregard, who was instructed to take the man's statement and not leave anything out, no matter how strange it seemed. Beauregard, for his part, gave a solemn nod and entered the interrogation room with a firm look of determination on his face.

Before Harris could issue any orders, a man in uniform ran up to her. "It's in the news."

"What's in the news?"

"They know we've arrested a suspect and they know there's someone else involved."

Harris cursed. "Campbell?"

The man shook his head. "Not this time. Langford's lawyer

went to the press himself. He's trying to paint Langford as the victim. He's trying to say someone else was pulling the strings."

"Court of public opinion," David said. "Son of a bitch. That'll be good for him."

"And bad for us," Harris said. "We gotta get to Baker before he sees the news, or he'll be in the wind."

"What should I do?" the cop asked. He looked young. And nervous.

"Get that piece of crap lawyer inside. I don't care if you have to throw him in a cell. Just stop him from talking. Do what you need to do. We'll figure the rest out later."

The cop mumbled a quick "yes, ma'am," and ran off in the opposite direction.

"David," Harris said. "I need you to go over to Judge Kominski's house and convince him we need a search warrant."

"It's Saturday. He's not going to be happy."

"I don't care. If you must, say we'll owe him a favor. We need that warrant."

"What are you going to do?"

"According to Bradley, his father is wealthy. He's a flight risk. I'm going to head over to his house and keep an eye on him. Stall if I have to. That's why you need to hurry."

"Adelaide—"

"David." She stared him down. "This is not the time to argue. Get that search warrant. I'll be careful, I promise."

David looked like he'd rather tie Harris to her desk than risk putting her in that situation, but he nodded his head, squeezed Cassie's shoulder, and ran down the hall and out of the precinct. By the time he got to the door he had his phone to his ear.

"Go home, Cassie." Harris made her way over to her desk. "You've been a huge help. I'll call you when it's over, okay?"

"Home? Detective—"

"You know, I'd get a lot more done if people didn't try arguing with me every time I told them to do something." Harris sat down in front of her computer. "William Baker. Come on, you piece of shit. Work faster."

Cassie looked down the hallway David left through. Elizabeth was standing there, allowing the other cops to pass through her unnoticed. She reached out her hand and tried mouthing something, but Cassie couldn't hear the words.

"Detective," Cassie said again.

"What the hell?" Harris leaned closer to her computer screen. "Jesus, Bradley wasn't kidding. This guy owns four houses in Savannah alone."

"Detective!"

Harris didn't bother looking up. "Go home, Cassie. I'll call you—"

"I know how to find him."

Harris stopped what she was doing and looked up at Cassie, who was standing at the edge of her desk wringing her hands. "Come again?"

Cassie took a step closer. Her thighs pressed into the edge of the desktop. "Elizabeth is standing at the end of the hallway with her arm outstretched. She's trying to tell me something. I think that something is where Baker is."

To her credit, Harris didn't question that Cassie was seeing the ghost of one of the murder victims. Progress, Cassie figured.

"How would she know that? She wouldn't have been taken there."

"Her heart was," Cassie said. "And her blood. Some spirits are tied to their bodies. And he has a piece of her."

Harris tapped her pen against her keyboard's space bar. "I don't know about this."

Cassie looked Detective Harris in the eyes. "It's going to take a lot more time going to each of his houses and hoping we get to him before he sees the news. This is the best chance we have of beating the clock. Trust me, Detective. You've got to."

For a moment, Cassie couldn't read Harris's expression. Her eyes were wide, but her mouth was set in a firm line. She looked down at her watch, then at her computer, and then at the other cops standing around them. No one seemed to be paying them much attention.

"We need to go out the back," Harris said. "We'll avoid the press. If they see me, they'll follow us and that's not a good problem to have."

Cassie nodded her head and Harris took off toward the back of the precinct. Cassie followed her through the maze of corridors until they were standing in front of an unassuming door leading outside. When Harris pushed it open, they were both momentarily blinded by the Georgia sun cresting over the roofline of the opposite building.

Harris recovered, then strode across the parking lot with purpose. Cassie had to jog to keep up, and by the time she made it to the front seat of Harris's unmarked sedan, the detective was already pulling out of the parking spot.

"Where to?"

Cassie pulled her seatbelt down over her chest and felt the buckle click in place. When she looked up again, she noticed Elizabeth standing next to the exit sign that led out to the main road. It was harder to see her in the broad daylight, she was translucent, distorted the world behind her a bit. But her dark hair was enough to make her stand out against the environment.

"There." Cassie pointed toward the road. "Let the record show, I've never done this, so I don't know how this is going to work."

"Noted." Harris gunned the car.

39

Cassie had never thought about what it would be like to try to follow a glitching, blinking apparition from point A to point B. But if she had, she would've imagined a scene close to their current reality.

Cassie knew Harris was trying to stay calm, but it wasn't easy being directed toward an unknown destination when your GPS was literally dead. Harris left her sirens off because she didn't want to draw attention to their pursuit. They had to fly under the radar which was difficult when they were making last minute turns and short stops, tires squealing hard, leaving swathes of burnt-rubber flavored air.

"Remind me to never let you convince me to do this again." Harris pulled onto the highway after almost missing the turn.

"You might change your mind if this ends up working out in our favor." The sharp turn plastered Cassie into the passenger side door.

"Unlikely," Harris replied. Her eyes never wavered from the road ahead.

Cassie kept her eyes on the road, too, scouting for a ghost. She didn't know what would happen if she missed one of Elizabeth's directions. Would she give up and disappear, or would she keep appearing in the middle of the highway until Cassie realized they needed to turn around?

"Anything?" Harris had had the foresight to hop into her personal vehicle so they could roll right up to Baker's house in an unmarked sedan without looking suspicious. The downside to that was she had to drive near the speed limit so she didn't risk getting pulled over. Harris would never be issued a ticket, but they could not afford to lose any time.

Both could feel the clock ticking away.

"Not yet." Cassie's eyes roamed from side to side. Every time they passed an exit, she would press her face against the glass and make sure she didn't miss Elizabeth glittering in the sun. "Wait. There. Next exit."

Cassie had barely spotted her standing just beneath the sign to start heading south.

Harris switched lanes without bothering to use her turn signal. Cassie saw the driver of a red Honda Civic flip them off as they passed, but Harris didn't care, if she noticed at all. She took the exit easy and hit the gas as soon as she was back on the straightaway.

"Where are we heading?" she asked Cassie.

"Beats me."

They stayed on I-95 past Richmond Hill and got off on 17. Every step of the way, Cassie would see Elizabeth at the last second and call out instructions to Harris, who would curse and turn the wheel to make their next direction.

"Fleming?" Harris asked.

They passed through the small town and stayed straight until Elizabeth appeared out in front of a church. She pointed down a road opposite her and Cassie called out the directions. A few minutes later they entered the boonies. They were driving along a street with farms on one side and deep woods on the other.

Cassie rubbed her arms. "I think we're getting close."

"What makes you say that?" Harris asked.

"I'm freezing."

Harris leaned forward to check the temperature on her dash. "It's ninety-seven degrees outside. The AC is on low."

"That's what makes me think we're getting close," Cassie said.

When she next saw Elizabeth standing at the end of a long driveway, Cassie knew this was it. "Turn here. Go slow."

Harris followed Cassie's instructions and let the car roll forward down a gravel driveway. The trees were dense here and the driveway had recently been dug out and filled in. The fill dirt was loose. Plumes of dust kicked up behind them. Cassie hoped to God they weren't pulling up to a dilapidated house. They'd have to account for every step they took while fearing the place would collapse on them.

But when Harris rounded the driveway's final bend, a beautiful green Victorian appeared as if someone had dropped it in the middle of the woods.

From the outside, it looked immaculate. There were large rose bushes lining the front of the house, all the color of red wine. A swing blew in the breeze on the front porch and the sun glinted off the windows on the third floor.

"Are you sure this is the right place?" Harris asked.

Cassie leaned forward and saw Elizabeth staring at her from the steps leading up to the front door. "Positive."

"I want you to stay in the car," Harris said.

A chill ran down Cassie's spine. "I don't want to do that."

"Why not?"

"Honest answer?"

"Yeah."

"I'm kind of shitting myself right now, and I'd rather have you in my sights at all times."

Harris laughed and smothered it. "You know what, fair enough. Text David. Give him the address. Tell him the second he's got a warrant he needs to bring half the precinct to this guy's doorstep.

Cassie did as she was told and looked back at the house. All the windows were closed and there was no car in the driveway. "Do we know if he's home?"

"Let's go find out," Harris popped open her door.

Cassie tucked her phone in her pocket and got out of the car. Another chill went down her spine and a pit hollowed out her stomach. Elizabeth took three steps backwards and disappeared inside the house.

"Great," Cassie mumbled.

"Did you see something?"

"Elizabeth went inside. I hope that wasn't a sign that we're supposed to follow her." Cassie shook her head, knowing that was precisely what Elizabeth wanted.

"We'll knock so he doesn't think we're trying anything," Harris ascended the handful of steps to the front porch.

Cassie stayed on the ground and when Harris knocked, Cassie had the urge to look over her shoulder to catch a glimpse of the activity inside. A breeze blew through the trees, but other than a few birds chirping and chickens off in the distance, it was quiet. Peaceful.

A nice place to be laid to rest.

When no one answered, Cassie said, "Now what?"

"We have to wait until we have the warrant to go inside." Harris was staring down one end of the wrap around porch. "But we can check out the yard. Come on."

They crossed the driveway and Cassie made sure to stay as close to Harris as possible without getting in her way. The detective didn't pull her service pistol out, but she kept her hand near her hip. Cassie wasn't sure if that made her feel better or worse. They both kept looking up at the windows around the house to see if anyone was watching them.

Cassie spotted the mounds in the yard first.

There was one to the left of the house, about twenty feet from the front porch, and another about ten yards to the right of the first. Several mounds dotted the yard in a semi-circle. A figure stood over the last one and when she looked up, Cassie recognized her as Sage, the latest victim.

"Oh my God."

Harris gripped the butt of her gun. "What?"

"The bumps on the ground? I think they're the hearts."

"I'm not going to ask how you know that."

"Sage is standing over there." Cassie pointed.

"I said I wasn't going to ask." Harris walked closer to one. "What I'd like to know is why."

Cassie shrugged. "Bradley said he was using the hearts in a ritual. Maybe it's like a protection spell? He had to bury them in the yard around his house?"

"Protection spell? Burying hearts? That's disgusting."

"I don't disagree."

"And what's he placing them in? What's stopping the coyotes from digging up the—"

Harris's mouth hung open; her voice replaced by the crunching of gravel at the same time. A blue pickup truck appeared around the bend in the driveway.

Cassie, glancing around the yard for a safe place, started to duck. "Should we hide?"

"No, we don't want to make him suspicious. He won't know we're cops right away. Once he gets close enough, I'll announce who I am. Stay behind me. We'll keep him close and try to get him to let us inside. If we can keep him talking, we can stall until David gets here."

Cassie was about to agree with the plan, but as soon as the truck pulled to a stop, the man behind the wheel jumped out. She only had enough time to catch a quick glimpse of gray hair and the scowl on his face before he pulled a shotgun and aimed it right at the two women.

Then he pulled the trigger.

40

Harris reacted before Cassie could process what was happening.

By the time Baker had gotten the shot off, Cassie was on the ground and Harris was on top of her. Cassie had landed on a sharp rock. Pain radiated throughout her arm. It dulled almost as the realization of their current situation slammed into her.

Another shot rang out and echoed across the plot of land and Harris rolled Cassie behind a thick oak and pulled her Glock out all in one swift movement.

"Are you hit?" Harris asked. "Are you hurt?"

"No, no." Cassie's heart was pounding. "I'm okay."

"Are you sure?"

"I'm sure."

Baker shouted from the driveway. It sounded like he was walking toward the house. "Who the hell are you and what are you doing on my property?"

"Savannah PD!" Harris shouted. "Stop shooting!"

"You shouldn't be here," Baker said. "Especially by yourselves."

"Savannah PD," Harris shouted again. "Drop your weapon and put your hands in the air."

The CHUNK-CHUNK sound of the shotgun was Baker's response. A few seconds later, he shot off another round. Splinters of tree and bark cascaded down over them as the round shaved off the right side of the tree they were hiding behind.

"Savannah PD—"

"I heard you the first time!" Baker pulled the trigger again.

Cassie screamed as a small branch landed on her head. There was a ringing in her ears, but she heard a door slam.

"He's inside." Harris was up and moving across the yard. "Call David and stay in the car!"

Cassie ignored the directive. She needed to stay by Harris's side. She bolted from around the tree and spotted the detective crouching low next to her car. Cassie slid across the gravel as she made a mad dash to Harris. Her thighs, knees, and shins burned as the small rocks scratched through her pants and dug into her skin. She pushed past the pain and pulled out her phone and dialed David's number. He picked up on the first ring.

"Cassie? How's it going?"

"Bad, horrible," Cassie whispered with a tremble. "He showed up and started shooting. You need to get here. Fast."

David pulled the phone away from his face and started shouting. When he returned, he sounded frantic. "Are you okay?"

"We're both fine. But you need to get here."

"Fifteen minutes tops," David said. "Stay on the phone with me, okay?"

"Oka—"

Cassie didn't get the whole word out before Baker fired another shot. It hit the ground in front of Cassie. She jerked back. Misjudging the space around her, her elbow slammed into the fender, rendering her arm numb from that point down. She lost her grip on the phone. It slid across the driveway, out of reach.

"Don't go for that!" Harris peered over the hood of the car.

Another blast rang out. The right taillight shattered. Glass and plastic hung in the air, glinting in the sun, then cascaded to the ground. Harris returned fire. The bullet shattered the glass in one of the first-story windows.

The man inside grunted.

"Stay here." Harris sprinted for the front door.

Without thinking, Cassie followed her, skidding to a stop as Harris kicked in the door and pointed her weapon inside.

"Go back to the car, Cassie."

"I can help!" she shouted. "Elizabeth will help us!"

Harris didn't bother arguing. She kept her weapon steady as she walked through the door. "I know I hit him. He's injured."

"Look." Cassie pointed across the room. Under a swath of blood trailing along the wall, was his shotgun.

Harris nodded. "Good catch, but don't get complacent. I'm sure he's got firearms stashed throughout the house. He might've switched it out for a 9mm or a .40, something easier to handle. It'd make sense if I hit him in the arm or shoulder." She aimed her finger at nothing. "Stay right behind me, Quinn. Watch my back, okay?"

"Okay." Cassie's voice was so high she sounded like a child. "You wouldn't happen to have another gun on you, would you?"

"If I did, would you know how to shoot it?"

"More or less."

"Not the confident answer I was hoping for, but no, I don't have another one. If you spot anything else, grab it. Fire poker. Baseball bat. Anything, got it?"

"Got it."

Cassie stayed right behind Harris as they made their way through the front entrance and into the living room. Cassie noticed how beautiful it was, with period pieces of furniture and original hardwood floors. But there was something off. Wallpaper peeled at the seams. Paint chipped, revealing an artist's pallet of colors underneath the freshest coat. While the house gave the appearance of being pristine, it was all fake, a cover up. No amount of paint and wallpaper could hide the evil that roamed the halls.

"Do you hear anything?" Harris whispered.

"No," Cassie said, "do you?"

Harris shook her head. "Do you see anything?"

Cassie was about to give the detective the same answer, but as soon as they stepped from the living room to the kitchen, she noticed Elizabeth standing in front of another door. Her face was a mask of determination and as soon as her eyes locked with Cassie's, she faded away.

"I think he's through there." Cassie pointed to the door. "And I'm guessing the basement is behind that door."

"What makes you say that?" Harris asked.

"My vision from earlier, remember? I saw a basement with an altar. Ten bucks we go through that door, we find it down there."

"I'm not in a gambling mood," Harris said, "but I don't think we have a choice."

"Can't we wait for backup?"

"There's most likely a cellar door that leads outside. We can't risk him getting away. If he disappears into the woods, we may not find him again." Harris stopped outside the door and looked around the kitchen. "Butcher knife is missing. He doesn't have a gun on him."

Cassie followed the detective's line of sight and pulled out a knife of her own from the butcher block. "What's the plan?"

"I need you to be my eyes, okay?" Harris looked at Cassie, who was thankful the detective looked much braver than Cassie felt. "He knows this house better than we do. It might be dark down there. I want you to use my phone as a flashlight, okay? When I look left, you move it left. If you see movement somewhere else, you call out the direction and shine the flashlight on it."

Cassie felt like crying. "Okay."

"We're going to be alright," Harris said. "There's two of us. Three if you count Elizabeth. We outnumber him."

Cassie blew out a huge breath and nodded. "Okay. Let's do it."

41

Harris twisted the door handle to the basement and pulled it open sharply. It bounced against the wall with a *thunk*. She stuck her head into the darkness and leaned back. When nothing happened, she did it once more.

"There's a bit of light down there," Harris said. "But it's still dark. Might be candles. Are you ready with the flashlight?"

Cassie held up the phone and pointed it forward. "Yes."

"Remember, stay as close to me as you can without getting tripped up. If you see movement, call the direction."

"Okay."

Harris waited a few beats to make sure Cassie didn't have anything else to say, and she stuck her head through the doorway one more time. "Savannah PD. Come out with your hands up."

When there was no response, she lifted her weapon and descended the stairs.

Cassie moved in tandem with the detective, making sure she kept the phone's light over Harris's left shoulder.

The wooden stairs creaked, each one sounding like a gunshot in the silence. Baker would know where they were, and Cassie was terrified he was underneath them, waiting to sever her Achilles and send her sprawling.

But Harris was unconcerned. Maybe it was practice. Muscle memory. She had performed the moves so many times, they just happened. She took each step at an agonizing pace, sweeping her head left and right, making sure every movement was purposeful. She would pause on every stair to stop and listen, but Cassie couldn't hear anything except water moving through the old pipes.

Halfway down the stairs, Cassie got a glimpse of the basement opening in front of her. Unlike the rest of the house, it wasn't finished. It looked old, more like a food cellar than an actual basement, and she was certain that this room was in its original condition.

The hair on the back of Cassie's neck tingled and she felt her skin crawling, starting from her ankles and going right up her back. More than anything else, she wanted to get off those stairs. She couldn't ignore the feeling that Baker was lying in wait, ready to pounce.

They were about three steps from the bottom. Harris started to take a step down, and as Cassie went to follow, she misjudged the distance to the next step. She stumbled, and knocked into Harris, who had to rush down the rest of the steps to stay on her feet.

"Sorry!" Cassie whispered. "I'm sorry!"

"Stay with me, Quinn." Harris looked to the left.

"I'm with you." Cassie turned the light in Harris's direction.

In front of them were rows of wooden shelves. They looked new and each one held various canned goods. It was quite a stockpile. There was enough food to last several months, if not longer. What was this guy preparing for?

Harris kept spinning, guiding the light to the staircase they had climbed down. Cassie didn't like putting her back to the room, but despite the invisible bugs crawling across her skin, she stayed connected to Harris.

At the very least, she knew that Baker hadn't been hiding under the stairs like she had feared.

Harris kept moving and as the light swept the room, Cassie saw the altar from her vision. Her memory of what she had seen was vague but familiar, almost déjà vu. She leaned closer to Harris.

"That's what I saw."

"Let's move closer," Harris whispered back.

The detective kept her head on a swivel and Cassie stayed with her. There was a door on the far side of the room, opposite the stairs. Harris wasn't concerned about busting her way through it.

They got closer to the altar and the smell made Cassie's eyes water. On top of the table were seven candles colored a deep blood-red, almost black. Four of them were lit, the other three remained untouched with fresh, wax-covered wicks. A dull, red glob sat in front of the four that had flames and Cassie knew, without a doubt, that it was a piece of the heart from each of Baker's victims.

"Shine the light on the wall," Harris said.

Cassie lifted the phone to look at the wall behind the table. Blood was smeared this way and that. It appeared random at first. Cassie's eyes took a minute to adjust to what she was looking at.

In the center was a square with four spokes leading to red splotches that formed a half circle on the outside. Surrounding that were the symbols Cassie had seen in her vision, but she couldn't make heads or tails of what they were supposed to be.

"That's the house in the center," Harris said.

Cassie nodded her head. The light moved with her, casting shadows around the altar. "And the dots are the hearts. But what are the lines?"

"Something to connect the hearts to the house," Harris said. "Maybe the blood?"

Cassie was about to open her mouth to say that made sense but saw something pale move in the corner of her eye. She was quick-witted enough to call out, "Left!" and wait until Harris turned to look before she shined the light in that direction.

"I don't see anything," Harris hissed.

Cassie breathed a sigh of relief. "It's Elizabeth. Jesus, my heart's pounding."

"I can't decide if it's better or worse that I can't see her."

"I would answer that question, but I don't want to offend the ghost who's helping us."

"What's she doing?"

"Right now? She's standing outside the door staring me down." Cassie blinked and Elizabeth disappeared. "And now she's gone. She wants us to go through the door."

"Then let's go through the door. You with me?"

Cassie gulped, but answered despite the panic rising in her chest. "I'm with you."

The two women made their way across the floor with measured steps. When they made it to the door, Harris guided a full three-sixty turn to make sure no one was behind them. Despite the chill still running down Cassie's spine, the room was empty.

When they turned back to the door, Harris held up her fingers and counted down from five. When she got to one, she reached for the knob and twisted.

The door swung out with more force than Harris pulled with, and Baker barreled his way through the opening and collided with the two of them. Light flooded the space from a dangling, swinging bulb surrounded by a metal cage hanging from the ceiling. Had he been waiting there the entire time? All three hit the ground. The phone slid across the floor in one direction and Harris's gun in the other.

Someone kneed Cassie in the stomach and she grunted against the impact. A flurry of arms and legs, the three of them tried to untangle themselves and get the upper hand. Baker was the first to make it to his feet and he must've known Harris was the bigger threat because he reached down with both hands and lifted her clear off the ground.

Cassie had a few seconds to register him and was surprised by how much his son didn't look like him. The older Baker was tall and broad like Bradley, but his features were light. His hair was almost white and his eyes a piercing blue. He wore jeans and a plain shirt and if she hadn't known any better, she would not have thought he was as wealthy as he was.

Or that he was a serial killer.

The biggest difference between William Baker and his son, however, was the mask of rage that the older man wore on his face. It was beet red and encased a violence that scared Cassie down to her bones. A sharpness to his eyes made her more afraid.

This man had orchestrated the brutal murder of four women and had been smart enough not to do the dirty work himself.

Harris's instincts to protect herself kicked in faster than Cassie's. The detective kicked out with one foot and collided with the big man's knee cap. He grunted but didn't release the grip around her throat. He tossed her against the wall and watched as she hit it with a thud and slid down in what seemed like slow motion. The second she tried to scramble to her feet, he struck out with a blow to her temple.

The detective crumpled to the floor.

42

When Baker turned on Cassie, all she could do was curl up in a ball and cover her head with her arms. She decided right there that she was going to start investing in self-defense classes again. She was tired of being in these situations without the proper tools.

But she did have *one* tool.

Cassie became aware that she was still death-gripping the knife in her right hand. When Baker leaned down to wrap a hand around her throat, Cassie swung up and drove the blade in between his ribs in hopes he would back away.

Baker howled in pain. Instead of backing away, he released his grip on Cassie's neck and pulled the knife from his side. Warm blood squirted on Cassie's arm. The knife clanked against the concrete floor. His hands returned to Cassie's neck, squeezing so tight she was certain that her head would pop clean off.

She looked around to see if there was anything within reach

that she could use to defend herself, but her fingers scratched against the cold and empty stone floor.

Elizabeth appeared next to Cassie looking more alive and vibrant than ever as she looked down on Cassie's struggles. The slash across her throat and the hole in her chest were still present and gruesome, but her eyes were focused, and her expression was one of determination.

As Cassie's world began to darken, the spirit launched herself at Baker with a scream so loud he heard it. He let go of Cassie and stumbled backwards. Cassie felt the explosion that followed. It was as though the walls had collapsed in on her.

And then two shots rang out.

Cassie scrambled backward and noticed Harris on her feet, holding her pistol at chest level, aimed at Baker. The man turned to the detective, shocked at the outcome of events, and grasped at his chest as two plumes of red spread across the front of his shirt.

He sank to his knees and fell onto his side. His arms, hands, fingers all twitched. His right foot kicked out at nothing.

Keeping her weapon at the ready, Harris leaned down to check Baker's pulse. Satisfied that he wouldn't be moving any time soon, she rushed over to Cassie. "Are you okay? Are you hurt?"

"I'm fine." Cassie propped herself up on her right elbow and scanned her body. "Are you sure he's dead?"

"Not yet. But will be soon. We're safe." Harris looked from Baker to Cassie with a confused expression on her face. "What happened?"

"What do you mean?"

Harris shook her head. "I don't know. One minute he was

on top of you, and the next, there was this god-awful scream and he let go. Hell, he opened himself up for a clear shot."

Cassie sighed at the memory. "That was Elizabeth."

Harris's face twisted up. "I don't know how I feel about that."

"Is it the idea that a ghost saved our asses or that you now have first-hand experience with a ghost?"

"Both?" Harris shook her head again. "Yeah. Both."

There was sudden shouting upstairs and footsteps on the floor above them. Dust sprinkled down on Cassie's head.

"Down here." Harris yelled up the stairs. "It's clear."

Thirty seconds later, the basement was full of police, and David was reaching out for Cassie and pulling her into a hug.

"Quinn, this is the last time I'm telling you this--" David fought for an ounce of breath "--But you've got to stop doing this to me."

"Trust me, I'm trying."

"Well, why don't you let me know when you think you've got a handle on this whole 'staying out of trouble' thing. Okay?" He redirected his attention to Harris. "You kept her safe. Good job."

"Honestly? I think Cassie kept *me* safe."

David looked confused, but Cassie and Harris exchanged looks and smiled. He shrugged and guided Cassie up the stairs and out of the house, with Harris trailing close behind.

The outside air felt warm on Cassie's skin and she tipped her face up to the sky and closed her eyes to soak in what was left of the fading Georgia sun. The humidity had relented. The air felt less oppressive.

She inhaled, letting the sensation fill her from top to

bottom. This was the purest form of freedom Cassie could imagine.

When Cassie opened her eyes, she noticed a line of figures off to the left. She saw all four victims standing at the foot of the mounds of dirt that covered their hearts.

Hannah Williams.

Jessica Tran.

Elizabeth Montgomery.

Sage Washington.

For the rest of her life, and perhaps even longer, Cassie would not forget those names.

Each woman looked at Cassie and smiled. Their bodies had a glow to them as they stepped forward and vanished into thin air. Elizabeth was the last to go. Cassie felt the woman's presence on her skin. She knew what Elizabeth was trying to tell her.

"You're welcome," Cassie whispered.

This, she remembered, was the purest form of freedom.

She felt Harris step up next to her. "Do you see them?"

"Not anymore." Cassie stared at the spot she last saw Elizabeth. "I think they've moved on."

"Do you know where they go?" Harris sounded as though she was embarrassed for asking. "You know, afterwards?"

"No, I don't," Cassie said. "I just know they're no longer stuck here."

"That's good," Harris said. "Right?"

"Yeah." Cassie smiled and warmth filled her entire body. "Yeah, it's good."

43

A few days later and the world had moved on.

The news cycle was kind to the Savannah Police Department, calling Detective Harris's actions brave and heroic as she took down William Baker. Harris was quick to thank the actions of her fellow police officers and everyone else who aided in stopping the people responsible for those horrific crimes.

Cassie had requested she remain unnamed, but it still felt good to hear Detective Harris say those words. Two of the victims' families also went before the cameras to thank the police department for giving justice to their loved ones. They could rest easy now that all four women had been avenged.

Plenty of people were disappointed that William Baker had been killed. He deserved all that the legal system could throw at him for the rest of his tortured life. Some said he got off easy. So, they turned their attention to Dr. Richard Langford. His lawyer tried to get ahead of any bad press by painting his client as a victim. However, the facts spread unimpeded, and despite being coerced into murdering, very few people were sympathetic to Langford's plight.

David was certain they had a strong case against Langford, saying that even if he was the puppet and not the puppeteer, he killed those women. Not many juries were going to take it easy on him, and given Langford's obvious lack of remorse, he wouldn't be helping his case when he got on the stand himself.

After the events at the Victorian, everyone had returned to the precinct together. Harris had delivered the news to Bradley Baker. The man took it well, all things considered. Cassie thought Bradley would have a lot of emotions to process over the next several years, but any pain that his father's death might've caused would be offset by the fact that he had orchestrated much more pain on many other people.

Cassie wasn't sure how these events would impact Bradley on a personal or professional level, but given his kind heart and compassion, she knew he would make it through. There was no part of his father in him.

Cassie was shaken up after the confrontation with Baker, but she felt calm now that she had done her part to help the four women move on to the next life. After Novak, she had forgotten what it felt like to be the hero instead of the victim, and she had let her fear consume her.

Nevermore, she swore.

The trick was to embrace the terror. To work through it. To be willing to confront it again and again. Cassie had decided that she wouldn't run away from her fear. She wanted to accept that it would always be a part of her life. It would propel her forward in whatever way necessary.

Most people hadn't experienced horror like she had. Over

the last ten years, she had come to experience that deepest kind of fear a person could have—the fear of death. Confronting serial killers and seeing ghosts didn't rid her of that anxiety. After all, she had proof that there was something after this life. But that didn't allow her to ignore the feeling.

And she decided to embrace that.

It wasn't a decision she came to in a single moment. She had been contemplating it since the moment Elizabeth showed up next to Cassie's bed, silently begging her for her help. For the duration of this case, Cassie worked through what it would mean to give her time and energy to the spirits that came to her for help.

She didn't choose this life. It came to her and demanded her attention. She did it because she could and, on some level, she needed to.

But now?

Now, Cassie *wanted* to. Elizabeth reminded Cassie of how it could feel to offer another person your hand. She had reminded Cassie what it felt like to help another person, despite her trepidation.

Cassie woke up one morning in the middle of the week with her decision made. She would do whatever she could to help whoever came to her, even if it meant facing her fears. Unlike most people, she had the resources and tools and abilities to do it.

Returning to work after everything happened was a strange affair. No one knew that she was so involved in the case, except perhaps George. He gave Cassie a gentle pat on the arm and wished her well. There was something about the sparkle in his eye that led Cassie to believe he was aware she had done her part to get to the bottom of the mystery.

Magdalena, on the other hand, was oblivious. She rushed into work the next day and asked if Cassie had seen the news. When she said she had, Magdalena went on and on about how horrific the world was and asked how some people could be so hateful.

Cassie let her talk, not wanting to give away that she knew all this had happened because one man had been afraid. Sure, he hadn't been a good person or a doting father, but it didn't happen because he was hateful. It happened because he didn't want to die.

The irony that his life had been cut short because of his own actions was not lost on Cassie.

Jason was privy to these conversations since they happened over lunch. He was quiet during them and Cassie wondered what went through his mind. He had seen his own fair share of death and dealt with his own anxieties daily, something Cassie took comfort in.

Cassie was brought back to the present by the chiming of her phone. She was in her bedroom, half dressed, and trying to decide what she was going to wear on her date in an hour with Jason. She had taken the initiative and told him she was able to help her friend and was free for dinner whenever he wanted to grab a bite to eat. A knowing look on his face, Cassie half wondered if he had speculated her friend was involved in the case. But Jason didn't say anything, so Cassie didn't clarify.

They agreed to get seafood and wine that evening at *The Pirate's House*. A bit touristy, but good seafood, nonetheless. And every once in a while, a random ghost would join her for dinner there.

Despite a long day of work trying to restructure the 19th and 20th Century Photography exhibit, Cassie pulsed with energy.

She was excited to go on her date with Jason. Despite being terrified of what it might mean for their interactions at the museum, she couldn't let her dread get the best of her.

Never again.

She skipped over to her phone and saw she had a text from her sister. It was a picture of her sitting on her couch by herself, eating popcorn straight out of the bag and drinking a glass of red wine.

I love date nights, don't you?

Cassie laughed. Laura had been complaining for days about how long it had been since someone had taken her out, so she was finally pampering herself.

At least you don't have to spend the entire night being anxious over whether your date is going to kiss you by the end of it.

Laura sent another picture. This time it was one of her dogs, Chewie, licking the side of her face. *My date didn't even wait till the end.*

He's a lucky man. Cassie then tossed her phone back on the bed.

For the fifth time that night, she walked over to her closet and touched every piece of clothing she had. She didn't want to wear anything too out of the ordinary because she didn't want to make a big deal. But she also didn't want to wear an outfit she'd worn to work a hundred times.

She groaned and turned back to her bed where she had already laid out three different contenders for the evening. She was ready to close her eyes and pick one, but she found herself stifling a startled scream instead.

The ghost of the little boy was standing at his post in the corner of the room like he had done for months. Cassie hadn't seen him since she'd spotted him outside Langford's house, after which she half-wondered if he'd show again.

And now here he was, like he had not left in the first place.

Cassie threw a t-shirt over her head and approached the spirit. He kept his eyes on her the entire time, unblinking like always. She inspected him, like she had so many times in the past, but she couldn't see any injuries or marks on his pale, translucent skin.

When she knelt in front of him, it was with a much more open heart than she'd ever had in the past.

"Hey." Her voice was quiet. Gentle. "I'm sorry about ignoring you for so long. For being angry. But I'm here. I'm ready to listen. Take your time. I'm not going anymore."

The boy blinked twice, slowly, like he was contemplating her every word. He opened his mouth and, for the first time since Cassie had seen him, spoke. His voice was quiet but clear.

"Sarah Lennox."

Cassie stumbled backwards. She couldn't tell what surprised her more.

That he had spoken to her.

Or that she had recognized the name.

Cassie Quinn returns in *Whisper of Bones*, available now! Get your copy now or read on for a sneak peek.
https://www.amazon.com/dp/B08MVJ7KZL

Join the LT Ryan reader family & receive a free copy of the Cassie Quinn story, *Through the Veil*. Click the link below to get started:

https://ltryan.com/cassie-quinn-newsletter-signup-1

LOVE CASSIE? **Hatch? Noble? Maddie?** Get your very own L.T. Ryan merchandise today! Click the link below to find coffee mugs, t-shirts, and even signed copies of your favorite thrillers! https://ltryan.ink/EvG_

THE CASSIE QUINN SERIES

Path of Bones

Whisper of Bones

Symphony of Bones

Etched in Shadow

Concealed in Shadow

Betrayed in Shadow

Born from Ashes

Love Cassie? Hatch? Noble? Maddie? Click the link below to find coffee mugs, t-shirts, and even signed copies of your favorite L.T. Ryan thrillers! https://ltryan.ink/EvG_

WHISPER OF BONES
CASSIE QUINN BOOK TWO

by *L.T. Ryan & K.M. Rought*

Copyright © 2020 by L.T. Ryan, Liquid Mind Media, LLC, & K.M. Rought. All rights reserved. No part of this publication may be copied, reproduced in any format, by any means, electronic or otherwise, without prior consent from the copyright owner and publisher of this book. This is a work of fiction. All characters, names, places and events are the product of the author's imagination or used fictitiously.

WHISPER OF BONES: CHAPTER 1

Detective David Klein took a moment to enjoy the AC before exiting his sedan and making his way to the crime scene in the warm Savannah sun. It was early November, but temperatures were still in the seventies and eighties, and he wasn't looking forward to spending more time in the heat than necessary.

Not for the first time, David wondered what it would be like to move somewhere cooler, somewhere quieter. Lisa would laugh at him for even entertaining the idea. "You love this city too much," she'd say. "You'll be here until the day you die."

She was right. Usually was, in his experience. Lisa knew him better than anyone else on this planet. She knew him better than he knew himself. If she said he'd never leave, he had no choice but to believe her.

But damn if he didn't want to get away every once in a while.

The last few months had been rough. Savannah had just gotten over a brutal serial killer, one that had killed by ripping the hearts out of young women and draining them of their blood. However, the killer hadn't been working alone. William Baker had been the true mastermind of the operation and he was now six feet under.

Good riddance.

As usual after a heavy investigation, life had slowed down. The world had gotten quieter. Decades on the force taught him cases came in waves. There'd be a horrific, vomit-inducing murder, and then a quiet crime of passion. Neither was ideal, of course, but if you asked anyone on the force, they'd tell you in no uncertain terms which one they preferred.

But they didn't get to pick and choose. And there was no telling what was normal anymore. Was it normal for life to be calm and peaceful? Or was it normal for life to be bat-shit insane?

He didn't care to think about those questions anymore. For the past few years, what mattered was getting from one case to the next. One day to the next. It was easier if he didn't think too far into the future. He could handle today. Tomorrow might be another story.

David switched off the vehicle and stepped outside. The humid air clung to him like a wet sweater. The hot coffee mug burned the inside of his hand, but when he took a long sip, that same heat refreshed his throat. It was worth the physical discomfort to have a few drops of energy in his bank.

As he usually did these days, David took stock of his body. His knees and hips were stiff. In his shoulder, a pinched nerve. A slight headache forming over his left eye. His feet hurt like something else, but nothing out of the ordinary. He'd be more worried if he woke up pain free.

With a deep sigh and the resignation that only came after

years of working as a homicide detective, David walked toward the underside of Harry S. Truman Parkway. The officer who'd called him this morning about a dead body there had mentioned he might find it of interest. Other than that, he was in the dark about the subject.

A few officers stood at the edge of the underpass, keeping a group of the homeless away from the crime scene. The Chatham-Savannah Homeless Authority did its best to make sure the camps never got too out of hand, but the Truman Parkway was a hotbed for individuals trying to stay cool and dry.

A female detective stood closer to the body, waiting for David to nod his way past the officers, one of whom lifted the crime scene tape for him. He ducked underneath it, stifling a groan as his shoulder twinged in defiance of the movement.

When he straightened, the female detective lifted a hand in acknowledgement, and David returned the gesture. He saw Detective Adelaide Harris around the precinct nearly every day, but they never had much time to say anything more than a simple hello.

He'd always liked Harris' work ethic and dedication to the job, but he was more grateful to her for keeping Cassie Quinn safe when the two came face to face with William Baker. Cassie had a tendency to throw herself into situations without considering an exit plan. Harris had gotten her out alive.

Harris offered a small smile. "Good morning."

"Is it?"

"Could be worse." She looked over her shoulder at the body. "Could be better."

"What've we got?"

Harris walked David over to the body. "Male. Mid-60s.

Strangled, legs crushed. Been here a day or so. We can't tell whether someone killed him here or dumped him. There's been too much traffic in and out from the homeless. We've got one guy, Randall Gibson, who says they didn't know he was dead right away. Just figured he was sleeping. Not sure how true that is considering the state of the body, but when they finally figured out the man was dead, most of them got spooked and took off for another area. Mr. Gibson reached out to the Homeless Authority. They called us."

David was listening, but Harris sounded further and further away the more she talked. "Strangled *and* crushed legs?"

"Yeah." Harris drew the word out in anticipation of getting to this point sooner than later. "That's why I called you."

"How'd you know—?"

She laughed. "I've done my research, okay? The name David Klein would be one of myth and legend if you weren't still on the force, proving to people that you're real. I was interested in what type of cases you'd tackled over the years, what type of cases you'd solved. What type of cases you hadn't solved. This one stuck out."

"That was over twenty years ago." David shook his head. "Are you sure it's the same?"

"No. Not at all. But I figured you'd be the one to ask." Harris waited for David to say something, but when he remained silent, she took a step toward the body. "Want to walk me through what you remember?"

David followed her to the man's still form. His hair was gray, as was his skin. He'd been dead long enough for the blood to drain from his face. He looked peaceful, but a deep bruise around his neck meant he'd suffered as he died. His crushed legs showed he couldn't have gotten away as someone had slowly stolen his life.

"In the early '90s," David began, "we had figured out someone was killing addicts around Savannah. Within a few weeks of being released from prison, they'd show up dead. Our perp dumped the first three in the ocean. They washed up on shore soon after, and it was easy to tell they'd been killed in the same way—someone had crushed their legs, then strangled them. And pumped them full of heroin."

"The first three?" Harris asked.

David figured she knew the answer to her own questions, but he played along. Explaining the details to her out loud would force him to remember working the case when he was still a rookie cop. Maybe he'd remember something critical that could help them now.

"We discovered the next four bodies while searching the woods for a missing girl. It'd been about two years since the three bodies had washed up onto shore. The perp didn't bury one deep enough, and one of our dogs had sniffed it out. We couldn't tell if the perp strangled him, but he'd crushed his legs, just like the others. When we kept looking, we found three more. Seven bodies total."

"And then nothing?"

"And then nothing." David gestured to the body at his feet. "Until now, I guess. Do we know anything about this guy?"

"Not yet. I'm gonna have the boys do their thing, but I wanted you to have the first look at the body and the crime scene."

David bent down to get a closer look, this time allowing himself to grunt as his knees resisted the movement. Harris said nothing, and he was grateful. Staring into the face of a dead man not much older than himself was enough to make him feel like he was on death's door.

He took in what he could of the body without moving it. The man had on casual clothes—jeans and a polo—and had no distinguishing features. He looked average, bordering on handsome, with a clean-shaven face. He wore a wedding ring on his left hand.

"It's been a while." He looked up at Harris. "But he doesn't look much like what I remember of the other victims."

"How so?"

"The three we found on the shore were malnourished. They were addicts and looked like it. This guy looks healthy, all things considered. And he's wearing a wedding ring."

"Were the others not married?"

"Not that I can remember, but we'd have to go back to the old case files to find out for sure."

"What do you make of the wounds?"

David turned back to the body. "Strangulation. Hard to tell without a closer look, but it doesn't look like the perp used a rope. Back then, we thought maybe he was killing people with a tourniquet."

"And the legs?"

David's gaze shifted to the man's lower body. Blood had seeped through his jeans, but even without that sign, it would've been obvious something was wrong. The knee on his right leg was out of place, and his left leg bent at a strange angle. Broken.

"Done to incapacitate the victim. Make sure they couldn't run away. Then the killer could take their time strangling them."

"So, it's personal?"

"Can't know for sure." David placed his hands on his knees and stood up with another grunt. "But seems likely. The killer was trying to send a message, we just never figured out what it was."

"Think this is the same guy?"

"I don't know. Feels similar, but that was over twenty years ago. It's been a damn long time since we had a body. We always figured there were more victims, but we never found them. So, why now? Why him?"

"That's the million-dollar question." Harris waited until David caught her eye before she spoke again. "You gonna call her?"

David didn't have to ask to know she was talking about Cassie Quinn.

"No," he said. "Not yet. She deserves as much of a break as we can give her."

WHISPER OF BONES: CHAPTER 2

Cassie didn't blink as she studied the ghost of the young boy standing in the corner of her therapist's office. She'd only been there a few minutes before he'd materialized, translucent and stoic. He brought a slight chill to the air. She'd been seeing him outside of her own bedroom walls more often as of late, but she still had no clue why. He had only spoken to her once, uttering the name Sarah Lennox, before returning to his silent watch of her everyday life.

His presence had become more comforting than not. After the ghost of Elizabeth Montgomery had replaced him, he had come and gone as he pleased, and she couldn't help but look for him when he wasn't there.

Where did he go when he wasn't watching her? Did he haunt other people? Did he have other objectives to fulfill? She would ask him these questions every once in a while, but he never responded. He'd just stare at her until she went back about her day.

"Cassie?"

The voice of Cassie's therapist, Dr. Rebecca Greene, brought her back into the present. The woman was in her fifties, with brown hair streaked with gray. She always dressed professionally in a monochrome pantsuit. She had at least three for every color of the rainbow. Her closet must've been so satisfying to look at.

Today, she wore a periwinkle blue pantsuit with a white tank top underneath. Cassie had seen at least three other blue pantsuits over the years, but this one was the palest. It made Cassie feel warm and light. It was the exact color of the Savannah sky on a cloudless summer day.

"Sorry," Cassie said. "What were you saying?"

Dr. Greene's smile was calm and serene. Her eyes sparkled behind her black-rimmed glasses. "I asked you how you were doing."

"Oh." Cassie laughed. "I'm sorry. I haven't been getting much sleep lately."

"What's been going on?"

"Um." Even after years of being with Dr. Greene, she sometimes felt strange about opening up. It was her fatal flaw. "I've been having this recurring nightmare."

"Want to tell me about it?"

Cassie shifted in her seat, glancing back over at the ghost of the little boy. Was it for reassurance? She wasn't sure. "It starts off with me driving a car. It's not mine."

Dr. Greene nodded her head.

"It's nighttime, and I'm on the highway. I can't steer the car. I keep drifting back and forth across the line, but no matter what I do, I can't control it. Then I see people in the distance, just standing in the middle of the highway."

"Do you recognize these people?"

Cassie nodded. "When I get closer, I see it's my parents and my sister. My parents look like they do now, but my sister is about five or six years old. She's pretty young."

"Is your sister often young in your dreams?"

"I'm not sure." How many times had she actually dreamed about her sister? "I don't think so."

"What happens next?"

"I get closer. It feels like the car is speeding up. I keep trying to step on the brakes, but nothing happens. I get so close that I can see the terror on their faces. My sister is crying and screaming. I try to swerve, but there's no stopping the car. Right before I hit them, I wake up."

"And how do you feel once you wake up?"

And how do you feel when... Dr. Greene had asked Cassie that kind of question thousands of times over the years, and yet it was always strange to analyze her own thoughts and feelings. She'd much rather keep her head down and carry on with life, but that didn't fix any of her problems.

"Scared." Cassie's laugh sounded nervous, even to her own ears. "Terrified, really. Sad. I'm usually crying or sweating or both."

"Anything else?"

"Regret."

"Hmm." Dr. Greene wasn't the type of therapist who kept a notepad in front of her to make notes on, but every once in a while, she'd make an affirming noise and pause, as if she were filing the information away in her mind. "Do you know why you feel regret?"

"Not really. I understand the fear and sadness, but not the

regret. I tried everything I could to stop the car. It wasn't my fault."

Dr. Greene pushed her glasses further up her face. "So, as long as you do everything in your power to stop something bad from happening, you won't feel any regret?"

Cassie smirked. Dr. Greene was good at asking questions to flip Cassie's perspective on a situation. "No, of course not."

"Regret is a good indicator that a situation may not feel resolved to you, even if you've done everything in your power to fix it. Sometimes these things are out of our control. It's what you do with that feeling of regret that matters most." She paused here for a moment and rested her chin in her hand. "When did you first have this dream?"

Cassie looked up at the ceiling while she thought. "Maybe a couple weeks ago."

"About the time you decided to see your sister again?"

Cassie's gaze snapped back to her therapist's face. "Yeah, about that time."

"Is it possible that these dreams relate to your anxieties about seeing your sister? It has been a few years, after all."

"It's more than possible." Cassie blew out a long breath. "Seeing her again has been weighing on me."

Dr. Greene leaned forward slightly. "How come? What are you worried about?"

Cassie decided to let it all out. "Oh, everything." She laughed. "We were close as kids, but it's been so long and so much has changed. Will we still get along? Will she still feel like my little sister? Will she treat me like I'm made of glass, like most people do once they find out what happened to me?"

"Have you asked her any of these questions? Raised any of these concerns?"

Cassie looked away. "No."

"Hmm. I'd bet Laura is nervous, too. You're her big sister, after all. She looked up to you when you were kids. What do you think she's afraid of?"

Cassie bit the inside of her lip as she tried to put herself in her sister's shoes. "Probably the same things? Whether we'll get along. Whether it'll be awkward. Whether we'll still feel like family."

Dr. Greene leaned back. "So, you seem to share the same fears. That means you have a middle ground, a common issue. And, as always, the best way to solve a situation like this is with—"

"—communication."

"Exactly." Dr. Greene's eyes sparkled again. "I knew you'd been paying attention."

Cassie tried smiling, but it came out more like a grimace.

Her therapist didn't miss a beat. "What else are you worried about?"

"I'm not the same person I used to be. She isn't either. My life is so different now. There's so much I want to tell her. So much I want her to know." Cassie's eyes once again drifted to the ghost boy. "But she'll need time and energy and a willingness to listen."

"Is there anything that has told you Laura isn't willing to listen?"

"No, but that doesn't mean she will be."

"True." Dr. Greene shrugged her shoulder. "But as much as we'd love to, we can't control other people's reactions. Or their emotions. Or their actions."

"That's stupid." Cassie elicited a laugh from her therapist.

"I don't disagree with you there. Life would be much easier

if we could predict how people will interact with us." Dr. Greene checked her watch. "We're almost out of time for today. Did you ask Laura if she'll be joining us next time?"

Cassie dropped her head. "No, not yet."

"Okay, well, no pressure. It's there if you want it. If not, I'm sure we'll have plenty to talk about."

"Don't we always?" Cassie shook her head. Even after a decade of therapy, there was always something to talk about. But her weekly routine with Dr. Greene was reassuring. She might not tell her therapist everything—like the fact that she could see ghosts and sometimes got psychic visions—but it was nice to talk to someone who wouldn't judge her, no matter how anxious her thoughts were. She owed her therapist a great deal of gratitude.

Dr. Greene stood and walked to the door. "When will you be picking up your sister?"

Cassie checked the time on her phone. "Four hours and counting."

She tried not to the let the dread that had built up in the pit of her stomach show on her face.

WHISPER OF BONES: CHAPTER 3

Cassie's heart drummed against her chest as she stood in the Savannah Airport baggage claim area, wondering if she would spot her sister before Laura spotted her. Her palms were sweating, and she felt dizzy as mobs of people shuffled back and forth, grabbing their bags and hugging their loved ones. Their collective body heat made the air heavy and oppressive. The noise was almost enough to drown out her thoughts.

How long had it been since she'd last seen her sister? Three or four years? Longer? She had returned to Savannah for a few days in the spring to visit her old friends. She hadn't even stayed with Cassie. But they'd met up for an awkward dinner. It was nice, but superficial.

This time felt different.

Laura was visiting *her*. She was returning to Savannah to be with *her*. The plan was to spend a long weekend catching up, getting reacquainted, and visiting some of their favorite spots in town. Then, they'd pack their bags and head to Charlotte to talk to their parents as a unit. It was time to change the relationship among all four of them, and it would start tonight with her sister.

Cassie caught a flash of red amidst a sea of blondes and brunettes. Laura's hair had always been brighter than Cassie's auburn locks, which made it easier to spot her in a crowd. When Cassie turned, she caught sight of her sister, who was making a beeline for the conveyor belt. It gave Cassie a moment to catch her breath.

For all her fears, Laura hadn't changed much in the last few years, not physically. She was a little shorter than Cassie, but more athletic. Tonight, she wore leggings and a long shirt with a pair of flats. A backpack hung off one shoulder, and as she leaned forward to grab her bag, her soft curls fell in front of her face.

Once Laura snatched her suitcase and set it on the ground, pulling up the handle so she could lug it behind her, she scanned the crowd and found Cassie's gaze. For a moment, the two stared at each other in shock, and then broke out in twin smiles.

Cassie waited until Laura pushed her way through the crowd, still nervous about what the next few days would entail. Once Laura was in front of her, she felt her arms reach out and pull Laura into a hug so tight her sister squeaked in surprise.

"Watch the ribs," Laura said. "I kinda need those."

"Oops." Cassie pulled back and tucked a piece of hair behind her ear. "How was your flight?"

"Not too bad." Laura shrugged and started making her way toward the door. "It's not that bad of a flight. I just hate sitting next to gross dudes who don't know how to refrain from manspreading."

Cassie cringed. "Ew. Have you eaten?"

"Yeah, they fed us on the plane. Surprisingly, not terrible."

Cassie drooped a little. She'd hoped to take her sister out tonight. The sooner they got back to her house, the sooner they'd have one-on-one sister time, and Cassie wasn't sure she was ready for that yet. What would they talk about? What if they got into a fight? What if they got along great and she ended up regretting not reaching out sooner?

Maybe her therapist was right about the true meaning of her dream.

Cassie spent the entire walk to long-term parking thinking about what she should say to her own sister, and by the time they'd reached her car, she hadn't said a single word. She popped the trunk and helped Laura lift her bag into the back.

"Damn, did you pack a bunch of bricks?"

Laura's laugh was a welcome sound. "Fifty pounds exactly. I was so scared it would go over. But I needed to make sure I had enough clothes, just in case."

"Just in case what? The apocalypse?"

Laura's smile faded. "Just in case I needed to stay longer than a week."

Cassie slammed the trunk and looked at her sister across the top of her car. A streetlight was out nearby and the darkness engulfed them, but she could still make out the sheepish look on her sister's face.

"Why would you need to stay longer?"

"In case Mom or Dad need me." Laura waited for Cassie to unlock the car doors and opened the passenger door, but stopped short of getting in. "Or in case you need me?"

Cassie slid behind the wheel and waited for Laura to shut the door before giving an incredulous look. "Why would I need you?"

"You know, just in case. I don't know Cass, I'm just trying to be helpful."

"I've been doing fine for years, Laura." Cassie barely contained the anger in her voice. She hated when people treated her like she had FRAGILE stamped on her forehead. "And maybe Mom and Dad will want my help. I live closer."

"It's not a competition." Laura rolled her eyes and snapped her seatbelt into place. "I'm just trying to be helpful."

Cassie took a moment before she responded. She knew she was being defensive. Unreasonable. "I know. And I know I have a long way to go to make everything up to them—"

"You're their daughter." Laura put a hand on Cassie's shoulder. "You don't have to make anything up to them. Besides, they'll kick us out before we can volunteer to help. God knows Mom doesn't want anyone to baby her, even with a brain tumor."

Laura's words didn't make Cassie feel better. She still hadn't talked to either of them. Cassie had pitched her and her sister's visit as a surprise, but the truth was she didn't want to give her parents a head's up in case they didn't want to see her. Or just in case she decided at the last minute that she didn't want to go.

Realistic? Maybe.

Cowardly? Absolutely.

Cassie stuck the key in the ignition and twisted. Her car roared to life, and the headlights illuminated the surrounding darkness. The gasp that left her mouth was automatic, and she didn't have time to cover her reaction before Laura jumped and followed her gaze.

"What? What's wrong?"

"Nothing," Cassie said. She searched for a plausible lie. "I thought I saw a cat run off. Scared me."

"Jesus, don't do that." Laura clutched a hand to her chest. "I thought we were being kidnapped."

Laura seemed to realize what she said as soon as it left her mouth.

"Cassie, I'm so sorry. I wasn't thinking. I—"

"It's fine." Cassie forced out a laugh. "You don't have to walk on eggshells around me. Let's just get home, okay?"

Laura nodded and turned back to the front of the car. Cassie followed suit, and once again locked eyes with the ghost of the little boy who had been haunting her for months. He seemed to show up more frequently outside of her bedroom as her sister's visit had drawn closer.

Was it a plausible connection or simply coincidence?

Cassie couldn't say for sure, and she wasn't looking forward to solving that mystery. She'd already lied to her sister, and they weren't even home yet. How would she nonchalantly ask Laura if she had any connection to a little boy who had died twenty or thirty years ago?

Cassie twisted in her seat and carefully pulled out of the parking spot, knowing there was no simple answer to her question.

ORDER *WHISPER OF BONES* NOW:

https://www.amazon.com/dp/B08MVJ7KZL

Join the LT Ryan reader family & receive a free copy of the Cassie Quinn story, *Through the Veil*. Click the link below to get started:

https://ltryan.com/cassie-quinn-newsletter-signup-1

ALSO BY L.T. RYAN

Find All of L.T. Ryan's Books on Amazon Today!

The Jack Noble Series

The Recruit (free)

The First Deception (Prequel 1)

Noble Beginnings

A Deadly Distance

Ripple Effect (Bear Logan)

Thin Line

Noble Intentions

When Dead in Greece

Noble Retribution

Noble Betrayal

Never Go Home

Beyond Betrayal (Clarissa Abbot)

Noble Judgment

Never Cry Mercy

Deadline

End Game

Noble Ultimatum

Noble Legend

Noble Revenge

Never Look Back (Coming Soon)

Bear Logan Series

Ripple Effect

Blowback

Take Down

Deep State

Bear & Mandy Logan Series

Close to Home

Under the Surface

The Last Stop

Over the Edge

Between the Lies (Coming Soon)

Rachel Hatch Series

Drift

Downburst

Fever Burn

Smoke Signal

Firewalk

Whitewater

Aftershock

Whirlwind

Tsunami

Fastrope

Sidewinder (Coming Soon)

Mitch Tanner Series

The Depth of Darkness

Into The Darkness

Deliver Us From Darkness

Cassie Quinn Series

Path of Bones

Whisper of Bones

Symphony of Bones

Etched in Shadow

Concealed in Shadow

Betrayed in Shadow

Born from Ashes

Blake Brier Series

Unmasked

Unleashed

Uncharted

Drawpoint

Contrail

Detachment

Clear

Quarry (Coming Soon)

Dalton Savage Series

Savage Grounds

Scorched Earth

Cold Sky

The Frost Killer (Coming Soon)

Maddie Castle Series

The Handler

Tracking Justice

Hunting Grounds

Vanished Trails (Coming Soon)

Affliction Z Series

Affliction Z: Patient Zero

Affliction Z: Abandoned Hope

Affliction Z: Descended in Blood

Affliction Z : Fractured Part 1

Affliction Z: Fractured Part 2 (Fall 2021)

Love Cassie? Hatch? Noble? Maddie? Get your very own L.T. Ryan merchandise today! Click the link below to find coffee mugs, t-shirts, and even signed copies of your favorite thrillers! https://ltryan. ink/EvG_

Receive a free copy of The Recruit. Visit:

https://ltryan.com/jack-noble-newsletter-signup-1

ABOUT THE AUTHOR

L.T. Ryan is a *USA Today* and international bestselling author. The new age of publishing offered L.T. the opportunity to blend his passions for creating, marketing, and technology to reach audiences with his popular Jack Noble series.

Living in central Virginia with his wife, the youngest of his three daughters, and their three dogs, L.T. enjoys staring out his window at the trees and mountains while he should be writing, as well as reading, hiking, running, and playing with gadgets. See what he's up to at http://ltryan.com.

Social Medial Links:

- Facebook (L.T. Ryan): https://www.facebook.com/LTRyanAuthor

- Facebook (Jack Noble Page): https://www.facebook.com/JackNobleBooks/

- Twitter: https://twitter.com/LTRyanWrites

- Goodreads: http://www.goodreads.com/author/show/6151659.L_T_Ryan

Made in the USA
Middletown, DE
09 January 2024

47495523R00176